YOU KILL ME

K. LUCAS

WAKE UP. DIE. REPEAT.

YOU
KILL
ME

BESTSELLING AUTHOR

K. LUCAS

EBook ISBN: 978-1-958445-07-5

Paperback ISBN: 978-1-958445-08-2

Hardback ISBN: 978-1-958445-09-9

Cover Design by Pretty In Ink Creations

Editing and Proofreading by My Brother's Editor

For my husband

CHAPTER ONE

When I open my eyes, my wife is sitting on my waist, hovering over me. Her long chestnut hair hangs down onto my face, brushing against my cheeks. She smells of vanilla and fresh air and all I want to do is breathe her in, to absorb every ounce of her.

Thunder rolls outside; rain patters against the window above our bed. I smile at her even through my sleepy haze. Kendra hasn't wanted to make love in ages. She has a thing for thunderstorms though, and I want to thank Mother Nature for working her magic tonight. Waking up like this doesn't bother me in the slightest.

I reach for Kendra's hips, eager to take her up on the offer. I'm almost shaking from excitement, like a damned teenager, but she pushes my hands away.

"What's wrong?" I ask, confused. I wipe the sleep from my vision so I can get a better look at her face.

She doesn't answer me, only grimaces.

In an instant, the breath is stolen from me. I gasp as something punches into my gut, robbing me of oxygen. My mouth gapes, but no words will come.

Kendra's eyes are cold, hard. Her arm reaches back.

There's a moment when the pressure eases, but then I'm hit again—higher, harder.

I stare at her with wide eyes as the life leaves me. "Kendra—" I choke.

"Don't," she says through clenched teeth, still hovering over me.

There are specks of my blood on her cheek. I want to reach up, to brush them away, but I can't lift my arms. I go numb as the blood drains from my body. The knife she's driven into me is removed and replaced again and again until I know no more.

CHAPTER TWO

I wake up gasping for air. One hand flies to my throat, the other to my stomach. I pat myself down, swallow a few times, then sigh with relief. *It was just a dream—worst fucking dream I've ever had.*

The room is still dark other than when lightning flashes. I see Kendra's form next to me, huddled beneath the blankets. I feel her weight on the bed beside me. I reach across to touch her, feel her for my own peace of mind.

"What is it?" she asks.

I freeze, my arm in midair. She's not asleep. *And I didn't wake her.* Her voice isn't raspy—she's been wide awake. *For how long?*

"Bad dream," I say, pulling my arm back.

She makes a noncommittal noise and shifts her weight. I settle back into my pillow, sighing again. I can't remember a time when a dream felt so real, and it's terrifying. The way her eyes bore into my soul, the way she almost snarled at me when she brought the knife down into me. I shudder, trying to block the image from my mind.

My eyelids grow heavy, slowly drooping down. I let them close, wanting sleep to come, wanting morning to be here already. All I need is to fall back asleep, and in the morning I won't remember a thing.

Kendra shifts again. I'm on the cusp of oblivion when she moves over me. Her long hair dangles in my face, tickling my cheeks and forehead. Her scent fills my lungs, that same smell that makes my eyes want to roll back inside my head. I think about grabbing her hips and a bolt of fear shoots down my spine.

My eyes pop open. She meets my gaze and then plunges a knife into me.

CHAPTER THREE

A *dream within a dream. That's all it was.* I stare at the ceiling, panting, disbelieving. I feel myself for any signs of damage, the memory of the very real pain still lingering. I'm okay—completely whole and put together.

Kendra breathes steadily beside me, rolled over on her side beneath the blankets. *Just like in my dream.* I move away from her, toward the edge of the bed.

Something about her breathing bothers me. I know it shouldn't—*it was just a dream...* but it's a struggle to even look at her sleeping form.

Is she having nightmares tonight too?

A yawn escapes my lips. I'm so tired, it's like I haven't slept in days. All I want to do is go back to sleep and yet—I hesitate. *Is it possible to have a dream within a dream within a dream?* God, I hope not, but who the hell knows? I've never experienced anything like this and I'm starting to think I need to just get up and start my day early.

The look in Kendra's eyes as she hovered over me—so cold, so *real. Twice*—I shudder again. There's no way I can sleep now. Not after that.

I give in to the urge to look in her direction. Just as my eyes meet her form, I see her hand slip from beneath the covers to scratch an itch. *She's pretending to be asleep.* She was awake in my dream—both dreams.

I gulp. Dread rises in my stomach, I'm on the brink of panic. I can feel the blood in my veins turning to ice.

Slowly, I reach across to my nightstand. I flip the switch at the bottom of my lamp, flinching at the sound it makes even though I know it's coming. I squint, preparing for the light in the pitch-black room. Nothing happens.

I flip it again in the other direction. Still, nothing. I lean over the edge of the bed, reaching for the plug that must've somehow been yanked free of the wall.

"What are you doing?"

I almost jump out of my skin at her voice next to my ear.

"Jesus Kendra, you scared me half to death." I find the plug —it's still in the wall. "Power's out," I say, easing myself back from the edge.

"I'm not surprised. It's been storming all night."

I swing my legs over the side of the bed. "I'm going downstairs to check the breakers. You want anything?"

"You don't have to do that."

"It's no big deal. I can't sleep anyway." I reach my toes out, trying to feel for my house shoes so I don't have to stand on the cold floor.

"It's not going to make a difference."

Kendra's glacial tone makes me freeze at the edge of the bed. My heart jumps into my throat and suddenly I couldn't care less about the slippers.

"Why not?" I croak.

"Because I already checked," she whispers in my ear.

Pain rips through my back. I cry out in a mixture of surprise, agony, and outrage. *No, no, no, this can't be happening!*

The knife she's used to cleave my back open is pulled free.

My open flesh screams in agony. I start to rise, to get away, but a blow comes again with so much force this time I'm knocked off the bed to the floor.

"Kendra!" I cry. "Don't do this." I can't move. I'm paralyzed. *Crawl, dammit, crawl.* Nothing works. My arms won't reach, my legs won't bend.

Kendra gets off the bed. She takes one step toward me and then another, prowling like a predator. As she approaches, a single thought consumes me. *This is real. I'm not dreaming. This is—*

My wife grabs a fistful of my hair, yanks my head back, and slits my throat.

CHAPTER FOUR

Sitting in front of the enormous vanity mirror, Kendra watched the women pamper and prep her hair and skin to perfection. She wasn't used to this kind of treatment, at least not to this extreme, but thought she could get used to it. Goose bumps ran up her arms as the brush ran over her scalp and down the length of her hair. A snag.

"Sorry," one of the women crooned. "Are you okay?"

"Yeah, it's okay," Kendra said, trying not to wince at the pain. If she squinted too hard, her mascara might clump.

Kendra watched the woman work her way through the tangle as gently as she could before continuing to brush the rest of her hair. She sighed inwardly, loving the pampering, but frankly—bored. She had another hour and a half of this at least, until the ceremony and would have to sit here in this chair for pretty much the entire time.

Her eyes moved to the corner of the mirror, where her wedding dress hung. A flurry of butterflies broke out in Kendra's stomach. She grinned—she couldn't help herself.

"Getting nervous?" Megan asked beside her. Kendra's maid of honor was getting the works too, but unlike Kendra, she'd hardly looked up from her phone.

"Not really," Kendra said. "More—excited."

"Good! You should be. Seth is the luckiest guy."

"I think I'm pretty lucky too." Kendra smirked, thinking Megan might be a little jealous if she knew exactly *how* good Seth treated her.

"It's your wedding day, so I won't argue—this time," Megan said. She looked up from her phone to smile at Kendra. "He's not going to be able to keep his eyes off you in that dress."

"That's the idea, isn't it?"

They both laughed before each picking their phones back up—Kendra to play a mind-numbing game to distract her from the anxiety and Megan to check Facebook.

AN HOUR AND A HALF LATER, Megan and the other bridesmaids were helping Kendra into her wedding gown. Kendra's phone went off, but she was too busy and had her hands full of dress.

"Megan, see who it is, will you?"

Megan looked at the phone and frowned. "Hang on a minute," she told Kendra before answering. She held the phone up to her ear, listening, her face slowly draining of color the longer she did.

"Who is it?" Kendra asked.

Megan waved her off, then walked into the other room. Soon, Kendra heard Megan yelling at the person on the phone.

"What the hell is going on?" she said to her other bridesmaids.

They shared a look with each other before distracting Kendra with other things. By the time the dress was all the way on, and the train was tied up, Megan was back in the room with a fake smile plastered to her face.

She huffed. "Sorry, that was just the caterer. It's all figured out now. Nothing to worry about."

"God, with all that screaming, you really had me worried. I thought something happened to Seth."

Megan's fake grin fell a little. She chuckled a little too loudly. "Right!"

Kendra stared at her. "Okay... so are we late? How much time do we have?"

"We... have a few minutes."

"Megan. Tell me what the hell is going on. A caterer wouldn't make you look like that."

"Nothing! Everything is fine, I swear."

Kendra turned to her other bridesmaids. "Would one of you mind grabbing me a shot of something? I have a feeling I'm going to need it."

They both shared a look with Megan, who nodded. "We'll run to the bar downstairs." They each gave Kendra a hug before leaving the room.

Kendra moved to the suite's bedroom to sit against the edge of the bed.

"You'll wrinkle your dress!" Megan cried.

"I don't give a damn, Megan. I know you're trying to spare me, but all you're doing is making me sweat. Tell me. Now."

Megan moved to sit beside her. She grabbed her hand and squeezed. "Seth—he's—missing."

"*What?*" Kendra stood with a jerk, beginning to pace the room.

"No one can get a hold of him. His best man and groomsmen, his parents—everyone's tried calling—he's nowhere."

"Did they go to the house?"

"Yes. They retraced his route just in case there was an accident—nothing."

"I can't believe this! I can't believe this is happening!" Kendra was about to run her hands through her hair but stopped at the last moment, remembering the hour and a half she had to sit in the chair. On the verge of tears, she blinked, trying to keep from crying.

"See, this is what I was trying to prevent. I shouldn't have told you!"

"This isn't you. This is Seth!"

"There has to be a good explanation. He probably made a surprise stop somewhere, that's all. He doesn't have reception, and he'll only be a few minutes late."

"What if he's hurt?"

"He isn't. He's fine."

Kendra choked. "What if he—changed his mind?" She couldn't stop the tears from falling now. *I hope this makeup is waterproof,* she thought. Then she thought, *If there's even going to be a ceremony today.*

"There's no way. He's a crazy guy, but not that crazy. No way he would give you up, and especially not without a word." Megan pulled her in close as Kendra broke down sobbing.

The other bridesmaids came back into the room with a bottle of rum and four shot glasses.

"Good thinking, ladies," Megan said. "A little prewedding party sounds like just the thing."

Two hours later, Kendra, Megan, and the other bridesmaids were drunk, their hair and makeup were ruined, and the suite was a disaster. Kendra's phone rang. She looked at the caller ID.

"Seth!" she answered with a slurred scream. "You have some kind of fucking nerve—"

"Kendra, where the hell are you? I've been waiting. Everyone is waiting."

"*You've* been waiting on *me*? You're the one who's—" She checked the time. "Two hours late to our wedding!"

"I'm down here at the altar now. Would you please join me?"

Hot molten anger flowed through Kendra's veins. She ended the call and threw her phone across the room with a scream. Her face flushed; her hands shook. She stared at the cracked screen of the phone that now lay on the hotel room floor.

"Who was it? What happened?" Megan and the others asked.

"That was Seth. He wants me to join him downstairs." She began to cry again. "He didn't even apologize."

When Kendra finished crying, Megan asked, "What are you going to do? You're not—"

"This has to be a misunderstanding," Kendra slurred. She was so angry she couldn't see straight but thought it might also be in part due to the booze. She wished she hadn't gotten so drunk so she could *think*.

Embarrassment filled her down to her core, possibly more than the anger. She wondered how she could still marry Seth after what he'd done to her today—supposedly the happiest day of their lives. Then she wondered how she could give up a life with him without knowing the reason.

A text came through the cracked phone.

Kendra, I'm so sorry. Please, come marry my dumb ass and

make me the happiest man alive. I'll spend the rest of my days trying to make you just as happy as you make me.

Kendra swallowed her indecision. "Do you think you can make me presentable?" she asked her girls.

Twenty minutes later, she was put back together. "Wedding March" began to play on the piano, and Kendra took her first steps down the aisle, ready to become Mrs. McKnight.

CHAPTER FIVE

My eyes fly open. My hands bolt to my throat. *Again.* I sit up in bed, staring wide eyed into the dark room. I turn to see Kendra. *Everything is the same.*

It finally dawns on me. I don't know why or how or *anything at all.* But I do know it's not just a nightmare. This is real. Somehow, I'm stuck in a loop—a fucked-up version of *Groundhog Day.* And my wife wants me dead.

I'm not going to let her kill me again. I scramble out of bed, holding my hands out to guide me through the dark. Lightning flashes outside, lighting up the room with a burst of light, enough for me to see the closed door.

"Where are you going?" Kendra asks.

I *knew* she would speak, but I still jump at the sound of her voice. When I do, my hand hits the lamp on my side of the table. It falls to the floor and shatters.

I cringe at the noise, holding my hands up to shield my face. Kendra's hand touches my shoulder from behind. I scream and lash out at her blindly.

"Seth!" she cries, her voice filled with confusion.

I stop with a moment's hesitation, making myself meet her

eyes. It's so dark I can't make out her features well, but the storm through the window is reflected in her eyes. Kendra's lips are pressed into a flat line.

"What the hell is wrong with you?" she asks.

"Don't kill me." I take a step away from her, leery of being too close.

A slight widening of her eyes. "What are you talking about?"

"You have a knife."

Silence.

I take another step back.

"How'd you know?" she asks, all false confusion gone. The cold has seeped back into her, dripping ice from every word. She's not even going to bother trying to continue lying.

The air is knocked from me as if her words were her knife. "Why?" I whisper.

Until this moment, I held on to the sliver of hope that maybe there was a mistake or misunderstanding. She couldn't *really* want me dead. Not my wife. Not after everything we've been through—all the *years*. We love each other, we were—*are* —the exception!

Kendra scoffs. "Don't make this harder than it has to be, Seth."

"Harder than it has to be? Are you kidding me? Kendra, what the hell is going on?"

She lunges at me, catching me off guard. I scream as the knife slices into my forearm. In the struggle to keep her back, I step on pieces of the broken lamp. Shards dig into my heel.

I stumble, crying out in pain and frustration. I try to limp backward to the door, refusing to show her my back again, but she's on me with a mission. Kendra swings her knife, missing once, twice, then—contact.

The tips of my index, middle, and ring fingers are sliced

clean off. There's a small thud when they land on the floor and I have to hold my stomach to keep from vomiting. Blood sprays from my open wounds that I now have tucked in close to my chest.

When I take another step back, pain radiates up my foot where the broken ceramic digs deeper in.

"Kendra, stop!" I yell.

She only growls at me and lunges again.

I dodge, but when I do, I step on a pillow instead of the hard floor. I'm thrown off-balance and as I falter, Kendra comes in for the kill.

CHAPTER SIX

She's awake, the power is out, there's a pillow on the floor. I flip the covers off my body and over Kendra's head, hoping to buy myself some precious seconds. Holding my arms out again for balance, I jump out of bed, not giving a damn about the slippers. With the adrenaline pumping through me, I can't even feel the cold floor.

"Seth!" Kendra cries.

I ignore her and keep going for the door. I twist the handle, expecting it to be locked, wanting to cry with relief when it's not. The door swings open and I rush through, headed straight for the staircase.

There are no windows near the landing, no lightning flashes shining through to light my way. The dark is even blacker than in the bedroom, and even my dilated pupils can't make much out. I'm so overwhelmed with a sense of urgency. When I hear Kendra's feet hit the floor, I stop trying to feel my way around and just *move.*

At the top step, the cat howls as I step on his tail. I scream in surprised outrage when he digs his teeth into the side of my foot. I'm off balance, trying to shake him off, trying to escape

Kendra as fast as possible. I reach for the banister but can't find the damned thing.

"Where are you going?" Kendra's voice is right behind me.

It's the final nail in my coffin—she doesn't even have to stab me this time. In my panic, I move away from her, but my foot misses the step. I fall backward down the staircase, landing with a broken neck at the bottom step.

CHAPTER SEVEN

The fucking cat!

"Kendra, why the hell are you trying to kill me?" I yell at the top of my lungs, bewildered and full of bitter fury. The memory of the terrible pain in my neck still radiating through my mind. I enjoy the sight of her startling almost enough to smile.

Kendra turns to me with a perplexed look that seems to be genuine. "I'm—"

"Don't even try to deny it. You've just killed me five goddamn times, and you won't stop!" Anger rolls off me in waves. I don't bother trying to rein it in—it won't do any good anyway. I'm stunned that not only have I failed to stop her from continuing to murder me, and that I keep waking up— not dead, but that I have no idea *why* she keeps doing this. It's time she forks over some answers.

Her jaw drops, and she flounders. "I've *what?* You're dreaming, Seth."

I bark a laugh. "Trust me, I'm not, but oh, how I wish I was."

"If I've killed you *five times*, then why aren't you dead?"

"That, my dear, is the million-dollar question."

She laughs in answer, a giggle that turns into full-blown hysteria. The situation is so ridiculous, so *crazy*, I could almost laugh with her. *Maybe if I wasn't the one being murdered over and over.* I'm sure she wouldn't be laughing if she was the one in the hot seat.

"Kendra?"

"I'm—" she pants, trying to catch her breath. "I'm sorry. It's just—" She wipes tears away and makes an effort to stop laughing but seems to be having great difficulty.

I've had about enough. I'm torn between trying to pull answers out of her and getting away while I still have the chance. I want to know why this is happening and how to make it stop—not just the murdering, but the loop. "It's what?" I demand, slamming a fist against the wall behind us.

Kendra's smile falls. "I thought for sure you had no idea." She brings out the knife. Lightning strikes, reflecting off the blade.

I scramble off the bed, but I don't run this time. My heart is about to beat out of my chest. A little voice deep inside is screaming at me, *Run, goddammit, Seth, run!* But I hold my ground, desperate to get some kind of explanation.

Kendra stays on her side, watching me. "I don't know how you found out," she says, sober now. "Did Nick tell you?"

My eyebrows shoot to my hairline. *Nick? Who the hell is Nick?* "What does Nick have to do with this? He knows?" I take a step back. "Are you having an affair?" My mind reels. First, my wife tries to kill me, and now she's having an affair. What's next?

Kendra gives me a grim smile and tilts her head like I'm obtuse. "As much as I'd like to answer all of your questions, dear, I think it's time for you to die." She stands and takes a step around the foot of the bed toward me.

"Whoa, whoa, hang on." I hold out my hands to her,

remembering the recent loss of my fingertips. I press them together just to make sure they're still there. "Just tell me why. Why do you want me dead, Kendra?" *Come on, give me something!*

Her lips press into a thin line as a flush creeps up her neck, so deep that it's visible even in the low light. "You know why," she hisses before lunging.

I dodge back, yanking the lamp off my bedside table and throwing it at Kendra's face. It hits, but I'm still too slow. She slices my chest with a scream. I yell, grabbing the comforter off the bed in a panic, and throwing it at her.

It's the only thing I can think to grab, but it works. While she struggles to free herself, I run for the door. "Shadow! Move, cat!" I cry, hoping he'll move before I step on his tail again.

He growls and hisses at the sudden noise in his space, but it works. He darts across to another room as I step down. I make it past the first few steps when I hear my wife throw the knife. I only have a split second to react, and I'm still too slow.

It slams into my back with a crushing force. I take my last breath at the foot of the stairs.

CHAPTER EIGHT

At two a.m., Kendra woke with the urgent need to pee. The pressure in her bladder was bad enough to make her cross her legs for a moment. *Okay, okay, I'm goin'!* she thought, rolling out of bed.

In the bathroom, just as she was about to do her business, she noticed the box of pregnancy tests sitting on the counter across from her. She and Seth had been trying to get pregnant since before they got married, and the box was a cruel reminder that it hadn't happened yet. *When was my last period?* she thought.

The pressure in her bladder was almost too much to fight. She couldn't remember when her last period was, so she grabbed the box, opened a fresh test, and did her business. The best time to test was the first pee of the day, or so they said, and Kendra wasn't letting this one go to waste.

She sat on top of the toilet seat lid, staring down at the pregnancy test, waiting for the results to show. A few seconds passed and then—two blue lines appeared. Pregnant. Tears welled up in her eyes. After trying and trying and *nothing*— she'd been starting to wonder if having a baby was in their cards at all.

Biting her lip, she looked back at the box filled with spare tests. *Just to make sure,* she thought, grabbing a second one. A minute later, it reflected the same results—pregnant.

Kendra couldn't stop smiling. She laughed out loud, not caring if Seth heard. She cried tears of joy, wanting to remember this moment, in the middle of the night, forever. *This* was the happiest day of her life.

The first thing she wanted to do was run to Seth and wake him up to share the wonderful news. Then she remembered he was off work tomorrow. She decided she'd do something cute and creative, something the baby would get a kick out of —something they'd remember for the rest of their lives.

Kendra took the two tests back into the bedroom, stuck them inside her nightstand drawer, and climbed back into bed. When she was lying down next to Seth again, she held a hand against her stomach, thinking of how she might tell Seth. She wasn't tired anymore, was far too excited, and didn't think she'd be able to sleep again. But, within ten minutes, she was out like a light.

WHEN KENDRA WOKE AGAIN, it was to cramping so severe she doubled over in bed from the pain. "No!" she screamed, feeling the wetness between her thighs, knowing what it meant. There was only one thing it *could* mean.

"What's wrong?" Seth asked, sitting up beside her. He saw his wife moaning in pain and flipped the blankets off her to see what was going on.

Bright-red blood was soaked through her pajamas and all over their sheets. Kendra wouldn't stop moaning and screaming. Nothing she said was coherent enough for him to understand, but he had an idea. He jumped out of bed, threw on yesterday's clothes, and went around to Kendra's side of the bed.

"It's going to be okay," he told her, scooping her off the bed, trying not to cry himself.

KENDRA HELD on to Seth's hand as the emergency room doctor examined her. She felt so weak—all she wanted to do was curl up into a ball and fade away. The pain medicine they'd given her helped some but didn't do anything for her heart. *My poor baby*, she thought. Then, *I didn't even get to tell Seth. I guess he knows now.*

Fresh tears welled in her eyes as the doctor asked her question after question.

> *Do you know your date of conception?*
> *When was your last period?*
> *How bad is the pain now?*
> *How much blood did you see at home?*

Kendra let Seth answer for her when he was able to but for the most part, she was forced to speak. She wanted to go home —to be *anywhere* else besides there. She was too ashamed to meet Seth's gaze. He kept looking at her, kept reassuring her, but all she wanted was to be alone, to just fall asleep and never have to face this nightmare again.

"This isn't your fault," the doctor was saying. "Miscarriages are unfortunately far more common than you would imagine, especially at such an early term."

"Is that supposed to make her feel better?" Seth asked, anger filling his voice.

"I'm only trying to explain that this is normal. I'm so sorry for your loss, both of you." She turned back to Kendra. "Most women go on to have as many healthy children as they want. A miscarriage does not necessarily mean you can't get pregnant again."

Kendra couldn't speak, could only nod, her chin wobbling as she fought back tears.

Seth stood to shake the doctor's hand. "Are we done here?"

"Yes. I recommend seeing your regular gynecologist, Kendra, if the pain gets worse or if the bleeding hasn't stopped within about a week." She handed Seth some paperwork filled with information he would obsess over for the next month and sent them on their way.

Seth took Kendra back home, changed their sheets, and helped her get cleaned up. They climbed back into bed together and he held her while she cried. "Remember, we don't have to have a baby," he whispered. "I love you, and I want to be with you. You are my family, whether we have a child or not."

Kendra knew he was only trying to comfort her, but in that moment, she wanted to gouge his eyes out. She fought to keep from screaming at him, from turning on him and behaving like a feral animal. She swallowed her anger, repeating what the doctor said over and over in her mind.

There's still a chance to try again one day.

CHAPTER
NINE

With all this waking up, dying, waking up, dying, the storm outside seems endless. I feel like I haven't had a minute of sleep, but I know that can't be true... *can it?* I stare at the ceiling with heavy eyelids, listening to the thunder rolling on the other side of the window.

My wife is having an affair.

Is that what all this is about? She wants me dead, out of the way for *him*? She finally found someone else to be with and is ready to kick me to the curb? Why can't she just ask me for a divorce like a normal person?

I turn over to look at her, bundled beneath the covers, *pretending* to be asleep. Only a few more seconds until she makes her move. *How things change.* Ten years ago, Kendra looked at me with such love and devotion. She literally lit up like a light bulb when I entered the room. Now, all she wants is my death.

Am I bad in bed? I don't think so—hell, she put up with me for this long. A thousand different things come to mind, things I've done wrong or never did but should've. Years of mistakes to make her turn away. Into the arms of someone else, completely content with me going away forever.

I need to find out who this *Nick* is. If Kendra thinks he gave me a heads-up, it means he knows what's going on. Maybe if I can find out why she turned to him, why she wants me dead, I can figure out how to stop this infinite loop.

"Seth? What's wrong?"

Time's up.

This time, I lunge for her. I don't want to hurt her—never that. But I need to get my hands on the knife. I catch her off guard, but the problem is—she's already got it in her hand. As soon as I'm reaching, she's cutting.

I scream as she slices my chest open, feeling the blood pouring out of me, seeing her being drenched in it.

I fall back, abandoning my plan. But it's too late. Kendra cuts me again, this time across my throat without so much as a word.

CHAPTER TEN

I don't know if I can get used to the torture of my throat. I sure as hell hope I don't have to. *She has the knife in her hand already.* I can probably overpower her—I'm twice her size and have the element of surprise on my side. But can I do it without getting injured? Without hurting her? I just need to leave this bedroom—

I haven't been able to outmaneuver her yet, and I'm starting to think I might not have a choice here. I love my wife, still, even now. But if it comes down to physically hurting her or being stuck in this situation—well, let's just say she's made the decision a bit easier for me.

Slowly, hoping she won't notice until the last second, I reach for my pillow. I clench it in both hands as tight as I can, so tight I almost can't feel it in my fingers. Then, before I can think about it, I lift up and slam it on top of her head.

Kendra struggles and screams into the pillow, but I keep her face covered. Her arms flail, and that's when I notice she's not holding the knife. She scratches into my arms, clawing with everything she has. Her nails draw blood, but I hold on.

A shock jolts through me at the sight of no knife. I look down at my hands, holding the pillow over my wife's face. A face I've come to know as well as my own. *She didn't have the knife.*

Is it really the same every time or are there differences?

I can't do this. I let go of the pillow to grab on to each of her arms. She's gasping, trying to catch her breath, shaking, trying to get me off of her. "Seth—" she chokes. "Don't—"

"Where's the knife, Kendra?"

"I don't—"

"Don't fucking lie to me!"

"How—"

I bring myself closer to her face. I say it again, slow and menacing. "Where is the knife?"

She clenches her teeth together. She doesn't want to tell me—that's obvious.

"If I wanted to kill you, I would've kept the pillow over your face."

The hate in her eyes cuts me to my core. "I dropped it," she says.

And I realize that nothing is different this time at all. She would still kill me—might yet. *I should've taken my chance when I had it.* "Tell me about Nick," I say.

She gives me that same look of genuine confusion and I know whoever Nick is, I need to find him. "Seth, let me go."

"Not until you answer me."

"I'm not interested in talking about Nick. I want you to let me go."

"Oh, but I'm *very* interested in Nick."

Kendra's eyes narrow slightly. She tilts her head. "Why? What do you want to know?"

It hits me that I might already know this Nick. Kendra seems more confused that I'm asking about him than that I know about him. I could be reading her wrong, but I don't think I am.

"You're having an affair."

"I'm what—"

"Just tell me how you met him and how long it's been going on." I know she'll never give me a way to contact the guy, but if I can track him down through however they met, I might have a chance. This is the only clue I have to go off of, so I'm taking it. Kendra's phone is on her nightstand somewhere but I'm not ready to let go of her arms to find it yet.

She's silent for a moment, contemplating. She looks like she wants to laugh or throw up, or both. Whatever's going through her mind, it's eating into my time. This is the longest I've stayed alive since the loop started and I have no way of knowing how long it'll last. I might keel over dead without her even having to lay a finger on me.

"Are you going to answer me?" I press.

"He's—Megan's husband. Don't you remember? You met him when they had that housewarming party for their first house. You drank a beer with him by the pool..." The tone she gives me simultaneously fills my heart with guilt for not remembering—and makes me want to strangle her—because now I *do* remember.

"I'm supposed to know all your friends' husbands?" I pretend to be clueless because I'm too ashamed to talk about having drinks with a man who's now screwing my wife. "What does he do for a living again?"

"He's a veterinarian."

"Are they still in the same place?" *I remember that house and exactly how to get to it...*

"No... are you serious? You don't remember me telling you about them moving?"

"Does Megan know what you two are up to?" I ask, ignoring the question.

"No—Seth, stop."

"Don't tell me to stop, Kendra. You have no idea what I've been through tonight, and God help me if you try to feed me another of your lies!"

She flinches back into the mattress, eyes filled with fear. I don't want to hurt her—never wanted to, not even knowing that she wants me dead. But I know she's going to keep denying the truth and not giving me any new information to work with. I might be able to still get away if I can get the knife. *But not if I don't slow her down.*

"I'm sorry," I whisper. Then I do the only thing I can think of. My hands tighten around her wrists. Kendra starts to squirm beneath me, but I'm too heavy for her to go anywhere.

I push her right arm down next to her side, pinning it beneath my knee. Both of my hands are now free to continue squeezing her left wrist—her dominant side. I keep squeezing and twisting, harder and harder. I keep going through the pleading, through the yelling, through the cries. I keep going until I feel the sickening cracks beneath my fingers and know that I've crushed her wrist.

Tears stream down the sides of her face into her hair.

"I'm so sorry," I say again. I bend to kiss her, but she turns away.

I roll off her and off the bed, bending to look for the knife. It's too dark to see clearly, but I want to find it.

I pat my hand across the floor, wary, not wanting to slice myself open. Kendra shifts on the bed. I move away slightly, still feeling across the floor. *Where is it, where is it?*

Her feet touch the floor in front of me, and it hits me what an idiot I am. The knife isn't here. And just because her wrist is broken, doesn't mean she can't kill me.

Kendra plunges the knife down into my back over and over, her screams ringing in my ears as the life seeps out of me.

From the base of the stairs, Kendra called up to Seth, "Are you almost ready?" She waited for him to yell back some smart-ass retort about how he was born ready and she's the reason they were always late everywhere.

No response came.

"Seth!" she called again.

Silence.

She checked the time on her watch and then decided to head upstairs to let him know exactly who the one making them late this time was. In the bedroom, she expected to hear the sound of the shower running or see the closet light on, but there was neither. Everything was turned off and quiet—no sign of Seth's presence at all.

Kendra moved down the upstairs hall toward the spare bedrooms and bathroom. "Seth?" she called, peeking through each doorway. She passed the cat lying next to the banister, licking his paws and fur. "Where's Daddy, Shadow?"

He meowed in response and kept licking himself.

Kendra moved back downstairs. *He wouldn't be in my office,* she thought, but it was the only room left she hadn't checked.

"Seth, we're going to be late!" she screamed, hoping wherever he was hiding, he heard her.

She opened her office door—no Seth. The memory of their wedding day came back to her. He'd disappeared off the face of the earth, no one had been able to get a hold of him or find him. "I lost track of time," he'd said, claiming to be taking care of a surprise.

The surprise in question—a secret honeymoon that she'd had no idea about—was an amazing gift, but Kendra had a hard time believing that Seth was just picking up the tickets last minute. She'd harbored a feeling since that day, even with everything that passed between them, that he'd really been having second thoughts about marrying her.

Now that he was missing again, she couldn't help but wonder if he was hoping she'd go to this party without him and that he'd say he *lost track of time* later on. *Where the hell could he be?* she wondered, looking out the front window.

She realized he was probably outside fidgeting with his projects, and yes, he would definitely claim to have lost track of time. Kendra went for the front door, and as she reached for the handle, Seth's voice came from the kitchen. "Ready to go?"

She spun on him. "I looked everywhere for you! Where were you?"

"You didn't hear me calling back?"

"No, I didn't," she said, feeling irritated. "Are *you* ready?"

He shrugged. "I was born ready."

THEY PILED into Seth's truck, heading for town. "What's the husband's name again?" Seth asked. "Rick?"

"It's Nick," Kendra said.

"Right. Nick. Was he at our wedding?"

"No. Remember, they were separated for a long time, then they got back together."

"I didn't know I was supposed to remember those details," Seth said, perplexed.

Kendra sighed. "Just remember, this is a big deal for her. She and Aidan never bought a house together. This is a bigger commitment for her than marriage."

"Got it," Seth said, thinking how glad he was that his wife's friend wasn't around much. She rubbed him the wrong way, and he thought the feeling was probably mutual. "And... Aidan was who again?" he added almost as an afterthought.

Kendra only smacked his shoulder.

THEY ARRIVED at Megan and Nick's home, housewarming gift and bottle of wine in hand. Megan was a social butterfly, so there were a healthy number of guests, enough to make it crowded inside the home. Seth and Kendra dropped their gifts off inside, then made their way through to the backyard, searching for her.

"Kendra!" Megan called from near the pool. She met them with a hug—even giving one to Seth.

"Congratulations," Seth said awkwardly, trying not to check the time on his watch to see how much longer they had to stay.

"Thank you! Isn't it amazing? I can't believe the deal we got!" Megan cried, glowing with happiness. She gestured to the man standing slightly behind her. "This is Nick." After a few pleasantries, Megan said, "Nick, why don't you and Seth grab a beer? I'll take Kendra to look around inside."

Seth smiled at the idea but looked at Kendra with eyes that said, *don't you dare leave me out here alone.*

Kendra kissed him. "I'll be back soon. Have fun." She headed inside with Megan as Nick took Seth to the outside bar to pour drinks.

KENDRA HAD ALREADY SEEN the house plenty of times, but that didn't stop Megan from wanting to show her around. When they were alone upstairs, Megan noticed how drained of color Kendra was, and how weak she seemed to be compared to her normal self.

"How are you holding up?" she asked.

"It's hard," Kendra admitted. "But I'm okay."

"Has the doctor said anything else? Gave any reason why this keeps happening?"

Kendra shook her head, fighting back tears. "I don't really want—" She cleared her throat. "Let's talk about something else."

"Of course. I'm sorry, honey." Megan took her to the bedroom suite where the sellers had installed a custom surround sound system connected to a dimming lighting system. "I don't know who wants surround sound in their bedroom." Megan laughed. "But Nick is sure happy about it."

Kendra smiled. "I'm happy you two made things work out."

"Me too. Now, let's grab something to drink." Megan led her back downstairs to the kitchen.

A FEW HOURS LATER, Kendra found Seth in the backyard exactly where she'd left him. Only now, he had a drink in his hand and was flushed from drinking alcohol all afternoon. She couldn't say anything—she'd probably had more to drink than he had.

Kendra joined him, reached up to kiss his cheek. "Ready to go soon?"

"Any time you are."

She smelled the tequila on his breath—it made her want to stick her tongue in his mouth, to taste it on his lips.

"You're giving me that look," Seth said low, eyebrows raised.

"Am I?" She smirked.

"Right. Time to go." He slipped an arm around her waist, suddenly in a hurry to get back home.

AFTER SAYING their goodbyes to Nick and Megan, they climbed back into Seth's truck. Home was only about ten minutes away. Seth kept looking over at Kendra with a sly grin, and she did the same—a silent conversation they both understood.

Just on the outskirts of town, a police siren went off behind them. Seth pulled over. A moment later, a police officer stood outside his driver's side window. "License, insurance, and registration, please," he said.

Kendra fumbled through the glove box for the registration and insurance cards while Seth pulled out his license.

Watching them carefully, the officer said. "You blew through that stop sign back there."

"Oh—I guess I didn't see it." Seth's face was scarlet. His ears felt like they were on fire, and he knew from the look on the cop's face that he was in deep shit. This wasn't just about running a stop sign. The cop could probably smell his breath from where he stood a few feet away.

"Been drinking today, sir?"

Seth fumbled for the right words. "No. I mean—yes, a little. We just left a housewarming party."

"Step out of the vehicle, please."

Kendra felt her world spinning out of control. Nausea rose in her throat as she watched Seth step out onto the pavement and undergo a sobriety test. She began to cry. When Seth was put in handcuffs, she broke down completely.

I'm in hell. There's no other explanation. This is my punishment, my eternity.

How many more deaths can I take before I go insane? I'm afraid to find out. I need a plan—a strategy.

Nick. Kendra mentioned that he knew about her plan to kill me. I need to get my hands on her phone so I have somewhere to start. Even if I can't find his number there, she'll have Megan's.

I turn my head just enough to see Kendra. *How am I going to do this without getting killed again?* The second I move, she's going to know I'm awake. She'll move over me with the knife in a matter of seconds, and she's fast as hell with that thing. Hurting her didn't work. I can't stand the thought of doing it again.

I don't want to, but I think the only thing I can do is wait this one out. I have to pay attention to the flashes of lightning and the distance between them and the thunder. If I count carefully, pay attention to Kendra's movements and exactly how long it is before she comes to me, I can figure out how and when to get her phone without getting killed again.

I've been so focused on talking to her, getting answers

from her lying mouth. She's never going to tell me what I want to know. All she's been doing is feeding me bullshit lies, and if I want to find real answers, I'm going to have to do it the hard way.

MY EYES ARE CLOSED but not all the way. There's just enough space to see without being obviously wide awake. I count in my head, one Mississippi... two Mississippi... three Mississippi... it doesn't account for the time that I was already awake, thinking about what to do, but it's going to be close.

When I get to fifteen Mississippi, a crack of thunder sounds like it could split the house in half. At sixteen Mississippi, lightning lights up the window and bedroom. I keep counting past three more lightning strikes that sound like they're on top of us, all the way to one hundred seventy-five Mississippi, and that's when Kendra moves.

Three minutes. That's all the time I have. It's an eternity, and it's a mere breath.

As she slips one leg over me and positions herself on top of my waist, I keep counting, hoping and praying I'll remember after death. Seconds pass in slow motion like I'm swimming underwater. I try not to confuse counting time with counting my heartbeats, but with the blood rushing in my ears, I'm sure I've messed up somewhere.

The scent of vanilla fills my lungs. Strands of hair tickle my lips. *It's almost over.*

I brace myself.

She's waiting.

Another five seconds... and nothing. I open my eyes to see her staring down at me.

She tilts her head and gives me that same ice-cold smile. "Hello, Seth."

At one hundred eighty-seven Mississippi, the knife plunges into me.

CHAPTER THIRTEEN

The moment I'm conscious again, I move. *One Mississippi... two Mississippi... three Mississippi...* Holding my breath as gently as I possibly can, I inch my way toward the edge of the bed. My hands are shaking as I ease the covers over me and I release my breath so slowly I begin to feel light-headed.

As far over as I can get without falling off, I chance a glance in Kendra's direction. *Eight Mississippi,* she hasn't moved as far as I can tell. *Thank God for memory foam.*

My teeth clamp down on my bottom lip as I sit up. Sweat beads on my forehead with the effort it takes to move slower than a snail. I finally make it into a sitting position at the edge, and I feel like I could weep when Kendra is still in the same spot. She hasn't shifted an inch, not even to scratch her nose.

I keep counting, waiting a few seconds before I move again. *Thirteen Mississippi... the thunder is going to hit soon.* One last breath, and I stand. I take a step and then another, balancing on the balls of my feet.

Sixteen Mississippi... where's that goddamn—

An explosion of thunder shakes me to my core. I wobble on my tiptoes, throw my hands out for balance, then settle again. Before I can even take another breath, I move. The house is still shaking from the impact of the boom, and the window above the bed rattles, covering the sound of my steps.

I have about a single Mississippi before the lightning lights up the room with me in it. I'm a step away—and it comes. A light bright enough to light my surroundings, bright enough for me to see Kendra's wide-open eyes staring at me.

My heart stops. A Mississippi passes as we stare at each other wordlessly. Her eyebrows are high—*she's wondering what the hell I'm up to.*

Now or never, Seth.

The flash of light is gone, leaving everything darker than before. I jump forward to Kendra's nightstand. I hear her move on the bed, but I ignore her. There's no time to look. My hands fumble across the top of the table, frantically feeling for her phone. *Where is it? Where is it?*

It's not here! I rip open the table drawer just as another burst of thunder hits. My feet tingle as the floor vibrates. A second passes, and the room lights up once more. I can see the drawer, see everything in it—the ChapStick, the lotion, the reading glasses, the charging cable, the hair ties, the book—*no phone!*

I stare into the drawer, dumbfounded. *It's not here.* Kendra always puts it right here before bed—*right fucking here!* I shuffle through again, just to make sure it's not lodged in the back. "Fuck!" I yell. I've lost all count of my Mississippis. The phone isn't here, Kendra—

The breath is knocked from my lungs. I look down to see the knife sticking out of my chest, my blood dripping from its edge. It disappears back into my body as she rips it from my back. I try to take a breath, but nothing works. My lungs won't inflate. I—

I inhale a few deep breaths, reminding myself that I can breathe now. *The phone isn't in the nightstand.* There are only two other places I can think of, and if it's not in either of them, then I'm shit out of luck. *It's okay, Seth. You don't need the phone to solve this riddle.*

Having the phone will make it easier to get a hold of who I need to get a hold of, but it's not going to be impossible to do without it. *Two more places—worth a shot.* The problem is that I don't know if my number of deaths is limited. What if there's a cap and once I reach it, I'm dead for good? *Better not think about it.*

I take a steadying breath and then lunge for Kendra once more. My arms dig beneath her, lifting her clear off the mattress to my delight and her horror. Kendra releases an earsplitting scream that could wake the dead—I flinch, but hold tight, flipping her over onto her stomach and bringing her back down into the mattress.

With her face pressed down into the pillow, I move on top of her, pinning her arms beneath my knees. She's wiggling and bucking, shouting muffled curses into the pillow, but I'm too busy frisking her to pay attention to anything she's saying.

Her pajama bottoms have so many pockets! How—why on earth do they make them like this? Three pockets checked, still no phone. I pass my hands over both her legs, pressing, patting in a desperate fury. "Where the hell is your phone?"

More muffled screaming.

I grab a fistful of her hair and yank her head back from the pillow. "Where is it?"

She sucks in air, and coughs, "I'm not—"

I press her face back down so I don't have to hear whatever lie she's going to spit out. *Dammit! This isn't working!* She didn't go to bed with the phone—wait!

I move her head out of the way to lift up her pillow. *Jackpot.* The knife—and the phone.

For a split second, I consider using the knife on her. It would stop her, might end the loop—set me free all in one fell swoop. My fingers tighten on the handle, thinking of the way I broke her wrist within my grasp. I can't do it. I can't bring myself to kill her just because she's trying to kill me. Hurting her was bad enough. There has to be some other way to end this.

Knife in one hand, phone in the other, I climb off the bed, releasing Kendra. She flips over to her back, eyes boring a hole into me. Her hair and clothes are mussed, her lips pulled back in a snarl more akin to a wild beast than my beautiful wife.

"Stay there, Kendra."

She doesn't respond.

I take a tentative step toward the door. She remains in place, as silent and still as the dead. I continue backward, never taking my eyes off her dark silhouette on the bed. My eyes start to adjust to the darkness, and then a flash of lightning sears into them, leaving me more blinded than before.

When the door handle is within reach, I use my hand holding the phone to pound on it a couple of times first in an attempt to get the cat to move. "Shadow, move your ass, cat!" I yell, then twist it open.

Once I'm through the doorway, I turn and run. My heart lurches when I take a few steps down the stairs without falling to my death. I keep going to the bottom step, expecting Kendra's footsteps to follow behind but not able to slow myself enough to listen.

Muscle memory makes me reach for the light switch on the entryway wall. Nothing happens. *The power's out! Stop wasting time!*

I fumble for the keys hanging on their hooks. *God, why do we have so many keys?* I make a silent vow that if I ever make it out of this alive, I'm going through the damned keys and getting rid of half of them.

My fingers brush a key fob. I pause to feel its shape and the buttons. A step creaks at the top of the stairs, and I grip the knife harder. I rip the fob from the holder, bringing half the keys down with it.

I press the panic button on the fob and the alarm goes off on Kendra's Dodge Charger. *Shit!* It's in the garage—no power. I can open the door manually, but for the life of me, I can't remember where I parked my truck. *Did I park in front of the garage door?*

Another creak comes—she's almost to the bottom. *Gonna have to hope for the best.*

I don't have time to wait for another bolt of lightning. Kendra is on my ass, and I have no way of knowing whether or not she has some other weapon up her sleeve. All I can do is make my way through the living room and kitchen with my arms stretched wide.

I touch the cold granite countertop, feel my way past the island, and make it to the garage door. "Seth?" Kendra says as I touch the handle.

I don't stop to chat. There's nothing she *will* say that's true or useful, so why waste more time? The door swings wide and I step down onto the freezing garage floor.

The Charger's flashing lights are bright enough for me to see my way to the manual pull string. The minute I manage to roll the door open, sheets of rain coming in sideways wet the cement beneath my bare feet. My foot slips, but I catch the hood of the car to brace myself.

I chance a glance out into the night. Pitch-black nothingness meets my eyes, sending a chill straight to my core. *Is this what I'm faced with forever?* Another lightning strike, accompanied by the flashing Charger lights, lights up the driveway, yard, and barn area. I finally have something to smile about when I see my truck is by the barn—not in the way.

As I come around to the driver's side, my foot slips again but I catch myself on the mirror. I pant, bracing myself on it. *All I need is to fall and break my neck now.*

I allow myself a quick look at the door that leads back into the kitchen. *Still shut.* Kendra hasn't followed me. *I wonder why...*

No time to think about it. I need to get the hell out of here to safety, somewhere where I can actually take a second to look through her phone. I make it inside the car, cut the mind-numbing sound of the alarm, and start the engine. *I can't believe I actually made—*

"Hello, Seth."

My stomach drops. Bile rises. I look into the rearview mirror and see Kendra in the back seat with a gun pointed at the back of my head.

"I didn't want to do it this way," she says with a shrug.

"Kendra, wait—"

She pulls the trigger.

CHAPTER FIFTEEN

Without missing a beat, I dive for Kendra's pillow before she has a chance to realize what's happening. I lift it with ease now that I'm not worried about her having the knife. It and her phone are waiting for me beneath, just like before.

Part of me was afraid they wouldn't be there—some cruel twist of fate would change the game, would prevent me from getting ahead even a little. Some force wants me in this loop, wants me to suffer for a reason, and whatever it is, probably wouldn't be happy with me finding my way out.

Filled with relief, I grab the knife and phone, hesitating only a moment. The thought comes back to me—*I could kill her*. I could end it now; how easy it would be. If Kendra's dead, this whole thing ends—maybe. And if not, well, at least she won't be trying to kill me anymore.

My fingers tighten on the knife's handle, growing slippery with sweat. I blink and shake my head. *No, I can't do it*. What kind of man does it make me that I keep thinking about this?

"Seth? What's going on?" Kendra says, agitated. She moves the hair from her eyes, stilling as soon as she sees the knife.

"Planning to do something with this, dear?" I drawl.

She transforms before my eyes into a cold, emotionless mannequin. "What are you going to do?"

"I'm going to get the hell away from you." I back my way off the bed, pointing the knife at her. "Don't follow me, Kendra. I'll use this if I have to."

She leans against the headboard, crossing her legs in front of her like a queen waiting to be served breakfast in bed. She doesn't attempt to move or even speak as I make my way across the room to the door.

As I rest my hand on the door handle, Kendra's fingernails begin to tap one by one on the headboard like she's waiting impatiently for me to move on. The slow, methodical sound sends chills up my spine, but it reminds me about the cat just in time.

"Shadow!" I call with a loud slap against the open door.

He yowls and darts across the landing in an invisible flurry. His nails claw into something hard—probably the doorway that he likes to ruin, but he's out of the way. I slam the door behind me and move with bated breath, part of me expecting her to tear after me any moment.

I take the first few steps cautiously, not wanting to fall and break my neck again. Halfway down, when I know even if I do fall, it won't kill me, I pick up my pace. At the bottom of the stairs, muscle memory kicks in again, and I stop to reach for the light switch.

Dammit, remember the power's out!

I move to the keys, shuffling through them as fast as I can. I've never had to do so many things in the dark before, but it's starting to grow on me. This time, I remember how many of the damned things we actually have, and there's no shock when I feel them all hanging there mixed together. My fingers brush against a fob and I latch on to it like a lifeline.

Just like last time, I press the panic button to set off the alarm. The Charger's horn can be heard through the walls, and I know which keys I've grabbed.

I make my way across the house to the garage door, moving as fast as I can. My hands out in front of me, remembering the same steps I took earlier, I manage to not hit anything on my way through. When I step down into the garage, the freezing cement floor sends a jolt through me.

Remembering my fatal mistake last time, I hit lock on the car doors, then I move faster, more eager than ever to get the hell gone. With the pull string, I manage to get the big door up, and once again, rain sprays in, soaking the surrounding floor. *It's okay... a little rain never hurt anybody.* I place a hand on the car to steady myself as I come around to the driver's side.

I take a few steps, slip, and correct myself. I keep going, knowing I won't fall, knowing there's no time to worry about —I slip again. This time I don't catch myself.

My feet fly out from under me as my hands flail, grasping for the car that I can't get a hold of. I land hard on my back, my neck and head whip back and when my skull hits the cement, I hear the crack from deep within.

I moan at the pain and close my eyes against the black spots that fill my vision. The car alarm is still ringing in my ears, pounding on my now aching brain like a drum. With shaking fingers, I reach for the fob again to silence the alarm. It leaves me in darkness once again, but the blessed silence is worth it. I allow myself a moment to clear my vision, wait for death to reset my day, and when nothing comes, I work my way up off the floor.

You can do this, Seth. Almost there!

Only a few more steps to the door. I stay low, on my hands and knees, to ease the pressure in my head and to prevent falling again. Rainwater soaks into my pajama bottoms, but it's the least of my concerns.

Finally, the door is within reach. I grab the handle and pull myself up into the driver's seat. The car starts beautifully, purring for me like a kitten. Panic shoots up my spine for a brief moment, as I remember last time.

My eyes shift to the rearview mirror. *No Kendra.* I whip around in my seat, scanning the back seat for any trace of her. *She's not here!* Breathing a sigh of relief, I shift into drive and take off.

THE STORM MAKES it harder to drive down the winding country roads, especially in the dark. I go slower than I'd like, squinting to see through the rain, swerving at the last minute around fallen branches that block my side of the road. The wind howls around me, fighting me, trying to push the car off the road—almost like something saying, *no, Seth, you're not getting away that easy!* I turn on the radio to drown it out.

Kendra's phone stares up at me from the passenger seat, waiting. *If I die again, I'll have to do everything all over and still not have a look at the goddamned thing.* I need to find a place to park, to finally look at it and get the information that I've been dying—literally—to get.

I reach for the phone. When I don't feel it, I tap across the seat with my fingers. *Where the hell did it go?* I turn my head for a split second to look—*there!* I grab it, turn back to the road, and my stomach leaps to my throat. There's a fallen tree across the entire road—and I'm about to hit it.

I slam on the brakes, holding the steering wheel in a death

grip. My body is covered in a sheen of cold sweat. My heart thrums in my ears. The ache in my skull is growing worse by the second, but I hang on for dear life.

The car's nose dives down, tapping the tree at the last moment before completely stopping. I wipe my wet hands against my pajamas and stare through the windshield at death that so wants to claim me. *Not this time, asshole!*

Kendra's phone is still in my hand, and I hold it up to my face to unlock it—muscle memory again. My face isn't programmed into it, so instead of unlocking, I'm prompted to enter a numerical password. I enter the code—nothing happens. I reenter it—still incorrect. *Shit!* She changed the password on me.

I try again, knowing I only have so many attempts before the phone locks me out for a period of time. *Incorrect again!* I slam the phone against the steering wheel, beeping the horn.

"Fuck you, Kendra!" I scream, hating her, hating myself for not thinking of this, hating life for throwing this insane curveball my way.

"Problem with the password, dear?" she whispers in my ear.

I scream, jumping in my seat, hitting my head on the roof of the car. I spin around to see my wife grinning at me, holding a gun that's pointed at my head. She's leaning over the back seat—that's been folded down. *She crawled through the trunk!*

"How the hell—"

She pulls the trigger.

CHAPTER SIXTEEN

My mind is still reeling. *How the hell did she get in the trunk? That sneaky*—my knuckles pop when I squeeze my fists at my side, pulling me back to the present. I wait. *Did Kendra hear the sound too?* The answer is most likely *yes*, but maybe she thinks nothing of it. I remember my Mississippis and have plenty of them before she makes a move.

As soon as it's clear she's not going to react to my knuckles popping, I reach for her pillow, ready to grab the phone and knife and get this show on the road. I feel like I'm in a video game, restarting the same level over and over, no pause button and sure as hell no save progress. How many lives I have is unclear—only that I have more than three. I only hope there's a way to win.

Her body leans forward with the pillow, but this time she doesn't cry in outrage. I grab the phone but my breath catches —there's no knife.

"Planning on doing something with my phone, Seth?" Kendra asks in a singsong voice. Hearing her speak is like nails on a chalkboard now—it's the sound of my fast-approaching death.

I start to scoot back, realizing too late that I've made a fatal mistake *again*. I waited too long to act, and, in this loop, it seems I have to move fast, without thinking, without breathing, without *anything*.

Kendra slices the knife across my chest, stunning me. A gash opens, the scent of my blood overpowering. I keep moving, but I'm too slow and she's too ready. She gets me again, this time stabbing straight into my heart.

CHAPTER SEVENTEEN

No time to wait, to think, to plan. Only time to act. Because if I don't, it's clear what will happen.

I get the phone and knife from under the pillow and force Kendra to look at the screen so I can unlock it. I allow precious seconds to get into the settings and keep the phone from automatically locking again. If it does, it'll be useless to me.

Unlocked phone in one hand, knife in the other, I leave the room, get down the stairs, and get the keys without tripping over the cat or otherwise killing myself. This time I remember my knee-jerk reaction to flip on the lights at the base of the stairs and I don't do it. It buys me mere heartbeats, but it's worth it to get out of here faster.

And this time, I *am* faster, leaving the house within a few minutes, with barely a hiccup. In the garage, I have no choice but to roll up the door with the pull string. I force myself to slow down over the wet cement and to take the time to check the back seat and trunk thoroughly.

I manage to do it without falling, only slipping once. Once I'm satisfied that Kendra hasn't made a surprise appearance, I get in the car, ready to get the hell out of dodge.

REMEMBERING the fallen tree that I almost rammed into, I leave the driveway in the opposite direction. I know I need to be cautious with this weather, but my foot is itching to press harder on the gas pedal to hear the roar of the Hemi underneath getting me far away from Kendra and death. The farther away from the house I get, the better, *more alive*, I feel.

Rain and fallen leaves spray my windshield. The wipers are on full blast, struggling to keep up. I keep the radio off, hating the sound of the gusting wind, but hating more the idea of Kendra back there somehow, preparing to pop out again and my ass not hearing her.

I'm forced to veer off road at times to get around fallen limbs, but there are no more downed trees. With no one else on the road, I have free rein to do what I need to do to keep going. It's slow going, but I'm finally able to breathe without the band over my chest when I see the town up ahead.

The first parking lot I see, I pull over. Kendra's still-open phone is waiting for me, and I finally have the chance to go through it. I want to scream out the window, *Finally! I'm alive and I finally made it!* But I don't want to jinx myself and I don't want to waste time, so I grab the phone and start scrolling.

Nick, Nick, where are you, Nick? I scroll to the *N* names on her contact list, but there's no Nick. I clench my jaw, on the verge of losing it again, but I start from the top again and work my way back down. He might be listed under last name first or his company name. Kendra said he was a vet—maybe that's where she takes the cat and has him listed that way.

I go through each contact, even the ones that are obviously

wrong, like *Seth*. It doesn't do me any good. There's still no Nick in her phone.

My fingers tighten around the chunk of garbage, ready to chuck it out in the pouring rain. *I might even drive over the thing —watch my wheels crush it into dust.* I stop, thinking of a new idea.

Megan. Nick is Megan's husband. I can get a hold of her, and from there, Nick will be a no-brainer.

With renewed hope, I scroll back through Kendra's contacts, almost crying when I see Megan's name, address— the new one, and phone number clear as a shining beacon in the night. *Finally, something is going right!* Without a care in the world for the time of night, I press the call button on her number.

It rings, rings, rings, and goes to voice mail. "Hi, Megan," I say, trying to control my shaking voice. "This is Seth, Kendra's husband. I really need to speak with you. It's an emergency. Please call or text back right away." I hang up and wait.

My foot taps against the floorboard as I watch the clock on the dash, 2:54 a.m. and not a soul awake in this town, on this miserable night, except for myself *and Kendra.* A minute passes, and then two. I press the call button again.

It rings, rings, rings, and goes to voice mail once more. *Screw this. I'm heading over there.* I don't have time to wait for a callback, to keep trying over and over, or to pause while she wakes up. *Nope.* I already learned the hard way—if I don't keep moving, I die.

Kendra will catch up with me, and she will end me. Every ounce of progress I've gained will be lost, and I'll have to start over from scratch. So, I punch Megan's address in the GPS and head in her direction like the hounds of hell are on my heels.

CHAPTER EIGHTEEN

I'm parked along the curb in front of a two-story Victorian that looks like it's been restored. I double-check the address on the phone just to make sure—*yep, it's the right place.*

Before I get out of the car, I try calling Megan one more time. It rings, rings, ri—

"Hello?"

I almost drop the phone. "Hello? Is this Megan?"

She sounds groggy, half-asleep still. "Kendra? Is that you?"

"This is Seth, Kendra's husband. It's an emergency—"

"Oh my god, is Kendra okay?" The sleep leaves her voice, replaced by cold dread.

"Yes, she's fine—"

"What happened? Where is she?"

"Wait—"

"I'm up. I'll get dressed—"

"Hang on!" I yell between clenched teeth. *This woman won't let me get a word in edgewise!* "I'm sorry," I say when she's silent. "Please, Megan. I'm outside your house now. Can I come inside to talk?"

"Oh. Oh, of course. I'll be right down."

I end the call with a huff and get out of the car. *I hope chatting in person goes better than this.*

As I approach the house, I brainstorm what to say, consider which approach might be best to take. If Nick knows about Kendra's plan to murder me, Megan might too. She also might not... but if I make accusations and screw this up, she might not be willing to talk to me at all. There's one thing I know for sure, and that's that Nick knows something. Whatever I accomplish with Megan—I have to get to Nick.

The door opens wide as I reach the front step. Megan is in a plush bathrobe and pink fuzzy slippers, hair in a bun on top of her head. Her eyes are wide and frightened, and she has her phone in one hand. And a candle in the other.

"Hi, Seth," she says.

"Hi, I'm sorry about the time of night."

"No, it's okay, come in." She shows me into the living room but we both remain standing. Setting the candle down on a side table and rubbing a hand across her midsection, she says, "I'm sorry the power's out. What's the emergency?"

"Kendra—" *Best not beat around the bush. She either knows already or she's about to know.* "Kendra tried to kill me."

Megan gasps like I just hit her. "She *what?*"

"I know, and I'm sorry to drag you into this mess, but she indicated that your husband might know something about it."

Megan holds a hand to her chest while taking a step back. Her mouth opens and closes as she struggles to find words. "Nick? No—no, that can't be right."

"She refused to tell me anything," I continue. "I had to get out of the house, get away from her. I need to speak with Nick now, though."

"I don't understand. Did you call the police?"

"No."

"Why not? I mean—it's okay. I'm sure there's some kind of misunderstanding..."

"Please, Megan. It's not a misunderstanding. I'm telling you, she tried to *kill* me, and your husband might be able to give me some answers."

She meets my gaze, and reality finally hits home. Her lips press together in a fine line. She bites her bottom lip and shakes her head. "He's sleeping."

I take a step toward the staircase.

"Wait," Megan hisses. "I called Kendra. She's on her way here."

I stare at her in disbelief. "How the hell did you call her? I have her phone." I hold it up as proof, more for myself than for her.

"I called the landline." She shrugs like it's an obvious answer. And it is—one so obvious, so ingrained in my reality that I forgot it existed. Kendra keeps an old, wired landline phone in her office downstairs. It's never been used but has always been there for this exact reason—emergencies.

I release a breath. "Okay. It's okay. I'll be quick." I take another step toward the staircase.

"No," Megan urges. "If she really tried to kill you, you need to get out of here. She's quick, Seth."

Don't I know it. "I still have some time—"

"No!" She sets the candle and her phone on a side table before putting her hands on my shoulders. "I called her before you called me! I got your voice mail and the first thing I did was call her!"

"How long?" I ask, feeling all color drain from my body.

Megan shakes her head. "Any minute."

My eyes are frantic, searching every corner of the living room. *She'll see the car outside. She'll be waiting. I have to hide. I have to get away. I have to talk to Nick!*

"Nick will be in the office in the morning. I'll tell him you need to talk. I'll make sure he knows." Megan grabs my arm and leads me through to the back door. "You can go out the back," she says. "Take Nick's jeep." She pulls a set of keys from a drawer and shoves them at me.

I stop with one foot outside. "Thank you for believing me," I say.

Megan gives a tight smile that looks more like a grimace. "I'll put her off. Just get away. I don't want anyone to get hurt."

"Megan—why *do* you believe me? Do you know something about this?"

She hesitates. "No, of course not. I can see it in your eyes that you're not lying. And why would you lie about something like this anyway?"

With a final nod, I turn and head down the back steps toward Nick's jeep. As I get inside and close the driver's door, a set of headlights is visible down the street. I duck down, waiting to see.

Within moments, Kendra approaches in my Ram. She gets out, leaving the door wide open for the rain to soak my interior. Her hands are empty, but she's clearly looking for me.

Kendra leans against the Charger's windows, scanning the inside of the car. She looks around, and I duck lower when her gaze lands on the jeep. Megan's muffled voice comes from far away in her entryway. Kendra calls back to her, and only after she's inside the house, do I pull away.

CHAPTER NINETEEN

I was so close. Nick was mere feet away, cozy in his bed, and all I had to do was push past Megan to get to him. It would've been so simple, so easy. I'm not that kind of person though, and she was trying to help—she gave me the keys to their car... *It'll be okay. I'll kill time until the morning, then I'll meet him at the office.*

PASSING the time is harder than I thought. It would be a perfect opportunity to take a nap, catch up on some shut-eye —I'm more tired than I think I've ever been. My eyelids are like lead just thinking about it. My head swims with the want of sleep, my body aches from the lack of it.

Even though I crave it, almost as much as getting out of this loop, I resist. What if I fall asleep and everything gets reset? I didn't make it this far just to do that to myself. No. I'd rather be tired—exhausted, than have to start from the beginning again, back in bed next to Kendra.

I drive around town for an hour, the storm and concentration it takes to get through it keeping me awake. On the other side of town, I find a place where the streetlights are still on and park beneath one so the light will help keep me up. Then I bring out Kendra's still open phone to do some more snooping.

THE STORM PASSES with the night, and within a few hours, dawn lights the world. Kendra's phone didn't hold much information for me, but it had plenty of games to keep me awake.

I check the jeep's center console and glove box, searching for some spare change or a wallet—anything that might get me a cup of coffee. There's a stack of napkins, a ballpoint pen, some rubber bands—my stomach clenches when I see loose change. I dig through the useless contents but only come up with less than fifty cents. There's not enough here to buy anything.

My stomach growls in protest. *I could go back home, grab my wallet, find my phone from the basket in the kitchen*—No. I can't risk it. Kendra would be ready and waiting—probably expecting me to do something so stupid. *It's fine. Who needs coffee anyway? Not me.*

When the timer on Kendra's phone finally goes off at eight o'clock, I start the jeep and head to Nick's office. He's one of two veterinarians in town, so his office sits off the main road. I circle the parking lot, making absolutely sure that Kendra's not going to jump out and stab me the minute I get out of the car. To my immense relief, the coast is clear. I park and head inside.

"Name?" the receptionist asks without looking up from her computer.

"I don't have an appointment. I'm here for a personal matter—"

"Name?" she repeats in the same cold tone, this time louder, more demanding.

"Seth. I just—"

"I don't have you in the computer." She finally looks up at me with an icy glare, frowning, eyeing me closely when she sees I'm in pajamas and have no pet in my arms.

"Like I said, I don't have an appointment. I need—"

"We don't accept walk-ins. You need to make an appointment before the doctor will see your pet." She scowls at my bare feet. "And *shoes* are required here."

"It's a *personal* matter. An emergency—"

"We cannot provide emergency veterinarian services here."

I grip the ledge of the counter so tight it groans beneath my fingers. I clench my jaw, trying to rein in my frustration with this woman. *How do they have customers at all with this lady working here?*

"Lady," I say. "I need to speak with Nick—"

"You need—"

"No! Dammit, stop talking over me. Listen to what the hell I'm saying to you. Go get him. Now."

Her mouth sags. She stares at me. Her tongue flicks across her upper molars as she thinks of something to say.

"Now!" I yell, making her jump.

She still hasn't moved from her rolling chair behind the computer, still hasn't grasped the concept that I'm not here for a damned *pet*. She finally starts to roll the chair back when a man comes from the hallway behind her. The woman stops in her tracks to bat her eyes at him.

"Is there a problem?" he asks, glancing from her to me and back.

"I tried to tell this person he needs to have an appointment, but he doesn't seem to understand. He's getting very upset and belligerent with me, sir," she says, all trace of her hard, forceful tone gone. She sounds like a young girl who's crying to her dad because her older brother pulled her hair. She looks up to him with large innocent eyes and back to me with a sly smile that he doesn't catch.

"You're the one who doesn't understand," I say. "I'm not here for an appointment. I'm here to see Nick on a personal matter."

The man's eyebrows shoot up. "I'm Nick. Can I help you?"

"I'm Seth—" I hesitate. He looks somewhat familiar, but it's been years. I try to scan his face for recognition, but I'm not totally sure. "Kendra's husband—we met before. At your housewarming party years ago."

"Right! Seth, of course. How are you?"

I give a tight smile. "Did Megan tell you to expect me?"

He frowns. "No. She didn't... come to my office. I have a few minutes before my first appointment."

"Sir, they're already here." The woman points to a woman sitting in the waiting room behind me, holding a small black dog on her lap.

"I'll be quick," I promise.

He nods and ushers me through the locked door, down the hall to his office. I don't understand why Megan wouldn't have said anything to him. She promised she would. She gave me his keys—I stop short in the doorway.

Kendra smiles at me from a chair in his office. "Hi, darling," she says.

"Such a coincidence," Nick says, continuing through the

room to sit behind his desk. "Your wife just came by asking about you."

CHAPTER TWENTY

My eyes dart between them, both full of smiles and sheer innocence. It's almost like everything that happened was a dream—never happened at all. *Was* I dreaming?

Kendra's smile is a little too wide, her eyes a little too bright. There are purple circles under them from being awake all night. Her fingers shake slightly on top of her lap. No. It was no dream. She's been waiting for me, and somehow she convinced her friend to give me up.

The two of them make a pretty picture—it's almost enough for me to gag. *She's sleeping with this idiot—possibly plotting my murder with him, and I'm just standing here, doing nothing.*

"Come in," Nick says. "Have a seat." He holds his hand out toward the empty seat next to Kendra.

I hesitate. If he is really in on Kendra's plan to kill me, or at least knows about it, I could be walking into the spider's web with eyes wide open. This could be exactly where they want me to be—the perfect place to end it.

"Seth?" Nick says when I don't move, his expression grows concerned. He looks between Kendra and me, finally grasping that there's something terribly wrong here. He doesn't seem to have the look of a man who feels guilty about anything.

"Do you think we can speak alone?" I say.

"Oh—" He glances at Kendra again. "Yeah. Sure. Kendra, would you mind?"

"Look, Nick, I hate to drag you into this," Kendra says. "The truth is, we're having some problems, and Seth is being rather childish. I'm so sorry to bring this to you at work. Would you give us a moment, and then I'll be happy to leave without a fuss?"

I start to shake my head. "No, Nick—"

Nick's patience with us is already wearing thin. Releasing a deep sigh, he glances at his watch. "I don't know what's going on with you two, but I better get to my first appointment. I'll check in with you after."

"Nick, please, wait. I'll only need a minute of your time—"

"I'm sorry. I have to go. I'll be back soon." He brushes past me as he leaves the room, and I'm left with Kendra once again. The door is still open; I can leave. She's across the room, still sitting—there's no way she can get the drop on me.

I'm so frustrated I could punch a wall. Nick was *right here!* And last night he was *right there!* How do I keep getting so close to finding out what I need to know and letting him slip right through my fingers? I should march down the hall and demand answers from him. I should—

"Join me, Seth. And don't be such a pussy. Shut the door," Kendra says, no longer facing me. She has one leg draped over the other, tapping the air with her foot while examining her fingernails.

It's not too late. I can run. I can get the hell out of here before she kills me again. Or—she might be willing to give me some real answers this time.

I do as she says, coming the rest of the way into Nick's

office and closing the door behind me. *She's not going to kill me here.* But just as I think it, I take a look around the room and notice all the things that she might use to do the job. I can't imagine her wanting to make my murder so public—she has to be concerned about getting away scot-free... doesn't she?

"Did you really think Megan would believe you over me?"

I come around Nick's desk to sit in his chair. I can face her now, with plenty of space—and objects between us. "She said she believed me. She helped me."

"She wanted you to get the hell out of there. Showing up at three in the morning, *threatening* her—"

"I didn't!"

"Oh, but you did, Seth. I had to convince her not to call the police. Convince her that you were going through a midlife crisis at the tender age of thirty-eight."

"You don't know what you're talking about, Kendra. She *offered* to help me. She gave me the keys to their car. She didn't feel *threatened*. She *believed* me, dammit."

Kendra folds her hands together and rests them in her lap. She quirks her lips and with a smirk, says, "Then what am I doing here, Seth?" She has that damned cocky attitude—the one I fell in love with, the one I absolutely despise now.

"Why don't you enlighten me, oh wise one? Please, put me out of my misery. Did you slice Megan's throat open before or after she gave me up?"

Her eyes narrow. "I would never hurt Megan. I'm not like you—"

"I didn't try to fucking hurt her!" We stare at each other in a standoff. It's still not clear what she's doing here, why she chose to meet me rather than wait for me at home. She must've thought I would go to the police, or she didn't want to wait for me to show up—I wish she would spill the beans and get this over with. "Why do you want me dead?" I finally ask.

"What makes you think that?"

"Gee, I don't know... couldn't be the knife under your pillow."

She flushes. "How did you know about it?"

And here we go again—a *second* seemingly endless loop, one of Kendra's making. She won't answer me, won't give an explanation. And when she does, she's filled with lies or mistruths. I want to roar at this woman, grab her by the throat and *make* her give me something, *anything* useful. Instead, I say, "You told me."

Finally rattled, she jerks back in her seat. "I did *not*," she says.

I shrug. "You did."

Her eyebrows dip low over her eyes but before she can speak, I say. "Is there a reason you wanted to talk to me? Why go through all the trouble to find me if you're not going to say what you need to say?"

Kendra reaches down into her purse that's resting on the floor beside her. When she stands, she's holding a gun. "You're right about one thing, dear. I'm not here to chat," she says, raising the gun toward my chest.

I push away from the desk, frantically scanning the room. Kendra is blocking the door. There has to be another way out of here, a way to get out of this.

"Are you insane? You'll never get away with this. You don't care about spending the rest of your life in prison?"

I move toward the wall on my right, where there's a second door blocked by a rolling cart. I push the cart toward Kendra, making as much noise as I can, and reach for the handle. It's locked.

"You're wrong, Seth," Kendra says. She grins at me, holding up something in her other hand that looks like a scalpel. With a swift motion, she raises it in the air and brings it down into her own chest.

I flinch. "Kendra, no—"

Kendra brings the scalpel down again, this time across her arm, holding the gun. She emits a high-pitched scream, crying, "Seth, no! You're hurting me!" Then quieter, she says, "Now, it's time for you to lie down and die." Before I can think, my wife pulls the trigger.

CHAPTER TWENTY-ONE

I wake up screaming, my hands flying to my face and chest automatically. *No, no! Not again!* I know I should be quiet. I'm wasting precious time, maybe even precious restarts, but the outrage is overflowing like a pot boiling over, hot and uncontrollable.

The sound of my screaming wakes Kendra. She sits up in bed, already holding the blade that reflects the storm through the window.

"Why are you screaming?" she says, sounding almost as frightened as me.

"You just killed me. *Again!*" I can't help saying.

"God, you scared the crap out of me."

Welcome to the club, honey. I remain silent, trying to catch my breath lying on my back, looking up at the ceiling. It won't be long now before she comes over here with the knife and finishes me off once again. At least I know it's coming. Two seconds ago—it was a bit of a shock.

Dammit, I was so close! I've been playing Mr. Nice Guy, even knowing what she's doing to me, knowing what's going to happen if I can't figure this out. I let her manipulate me. I let Megan and Nick dictate the timing. I even let the damned secretary have her say. Well, no more Mr. Nice Guy. I'm tired of playing games, tired of rolling over even when I know my death is imminent when Kendra's in the room.

From now on, I'm going to do what I need to do, even if it makes me an asshole. I'm going to—

Leaning over me, Kendra plunges the knife into my chest in a single, clean motion.

CHAPTER
TWENTY-TWO

The moment I'm reset, I move. I know the motions by heart now, know which way to turn Kendra to get under her pillow, know which side of it the knife's handle is, know at exactly which moment she'll flinch, she'll speak, she'll scratch that little spot at the back of her head. I don't even have to think about the Mississippis it takes for lightning to flash. They come, they go, the room lights, it darkens again.

It feels like second nature to get out of her grasp, out of her way, and down the stairs to the keys. With as many times as I've died, I would be a little worried by now if I haven't at least figured this much out. And as many times as I've done this, I know *this* is the part where things get a little sticky.

Move, move, move! Not going fast enough, Seth! the little voice in my head screams, knowing that Kendra is always one step behind me, right around the corner, waiting to slice me wide open like a Thanksgiving turkey.

At the keys, I fight my instinct to go faster. I slow down to get a better feel. My fingers brush along them, flicking through until I brush against the familiar fob to the Charger. I grasp it, tap the panic, but stay put. I keep feeling through the keys, until finally, I find my truck's fob.

This time, I don't cross the living room and kitchen to the garage door. I don't have to worry about manually opening the rolling door, or slipping—and falling on the wet cement, or having Kendra jump out from the back seat and shooting me in the head. None of that matters now, because I have *both* sets of keys, and I can walk right through the front door. Having to find the Charger's spare will hopefully slow her down enough.

My heart swells in my chest, pumping blood so fast I almost feel faint. I get to my Ram and could practically jump for joy. The feeling of *winning*, of actually doing something right, of somehow outmaneuvering my brilliant wife who seems to always be one step—or ten ahead—I nearly want to call back to her just to rub it in.

I push the feeling aside for now. There will be time enough for that later—*maybe, if I ever make it out of this loop.* For now, there are more pieces to the puzzle, and I'm just getting started. Now that I'm finally out of the house, there's only one place for me to go. I shift into drive and set the course for Megan and Nick's.

I KNOW BETTER than to call Megan again. Last time, the first thing she did was call Kendra when she got my voice mail, and I'm not making that mistake again. I can't blame her—it's her friend. She'd be concerned. Yeah, I get it. But knowing how easily she let Kendra talk her into doing her bidding—I'm not going there again.

Deciding a surprise visit will buy me more time—they won't be able to call Kendra first—I park and get out into the pouring rain, dashing up the walk to the front door. Beneath the stoop, I pound on the door. "Megan! Nick!" I call over and over. I keep beating my fist against the door and even on the glass of the entry window next to it.

A dog barks in the distance, but there's no movement inside. *Come on, no one can sleep through all this!* "It's an emergency!" I yell, cupping my hands over my mouth to make my voice carry. I try hitting the door again, and finally, the outside light above my head turns on.

A few moments later, the door swings open. Nick stands in the entryway, scratching his mussed hair with one hand, holding a baseball bat in the other. "Do I know you? What in God's name is going on out here?" He squints through the dark, realizing I'm familiar but also not quite picking up who I am in such low light.

"I'm Seth," I say. "Nick. It's an emergency, life or death—"

With a sigh, Nick lowers the bat. "I don't do emergency services. Look, I don't know how you got my home address—"

"It's not for a fucking pet!" I cry.

He grips the bat a little tighter at my outburst.

"Look, I'm sorry. Please, I'm having a very—I'm having a hard night. I need to talk to you. You're the only one who can help."

Nick takes a step back from the doorway, ready to either slam the door in my face or call the cops. "What's this about?" he asks cautiously. "It's the middle of the night."

"I'm Kendra's husband," I blurt, half hoping it explains everything. He knows her plan, he should know who I am just by her name and know exactly why I'm here.

And he does seem to look at me with a fresh perspective.

Nick lowers the bat and opens the door wider. "Come in," he says.

I follow him into the same room that Megan led me to earlier. I follow his lead, taking a seat on the couch, feeling too antsy to relax. My foot taps against the carpet in a rapid, anxious beat, drawing Nick's gaze. "Can we make this quick, if you don't mind? I think you scared my wife half to death."

"Right. I'm sorry about that. Look—I don't know how else to say this. Kendra tried to kill me in my sleep."

"She *what?*"

"I managed to stop her, obviously, and she asked me if Nick told me." I hold up my hands in innocence. "That's why I'm here. To get the details, to find out what you know— anything and everything. I don't even care about the affair at this point. I mean, I do, of course, but I can look past it *for now* if you can just help me figure out why the hell my wife wants me dead and how to stop her."

Nick stares at me, dumbfounded. He fumbles with his words, stutters, starts and stops. Finally, he takes a steadying breath. "Let's get a few things straight," he says. "One, I don't know anything about Kendra wanting to kill you. Two, I'm definitely *not* having an affair with her, and three, you stop her by calling the *police!*" His voice is steadily growing louder, and his final word is nearly a high-pitched shriek.

I cringe. "Keep it down, would you?"

He huffs. "Of course, I'm sorry. It's just—these are serious, life-altering accusations, my friend. If anyone heard them—I could lose my business, my wife..." He adjusts himself in his seat, clearly flustered and embarrassed, and part of me wants to believe him. My wife may be a pathological liar, but this man doesn't strike me as such.

"Why would she mention your name?" I ask.

"Has it occurred to you that she may know more than one *Nick*?"

"She specifically reminded me of who you were—that we met at your housewarming party years ago. Yours and Megan's first house together."

"Perhaps she's trying to steer you in the wrong direction? Don't take this the wrong way, but if she's really trying to kill you, it seems moot to give you the name of her true coconspirator." He frowns. "I have no idea why your wife would try to kill you. Money? Love? Revenge?" He shrugs. "I wish I could help."

I stand abruptly, no longer able to remain sitting. The tension is too much to bear. I need to pace, to walk, to *think*. He's right, of course. Why on earth would Kendra give up her true coconspirator? But also, why would he admit to being such?

I take another look at Nick, holding the bat a little tighter once again. He seems too—*something*. Maybe it's my ego, my pride, but I don't see her having an affair with this man.

"You're not sleeping with her?" I ask, needing to hear the words again.

"No. I swear it—I'm not."

Fuck! I believe him. Dammit, what do I do now?

Nick hesitates before asking. "Why haven't you called the police?"

"I can't do that to her."

"She's trying to murder you. Don't you think—"

"No."

He pinches his lips, clearly disagreeing, but he gets the picture. It's not open for debate.

"I can't put her behind bars. Yes, I'm sure I'm an idiot. But I just—part of me knows I can make this right. If I can just figure out *why* and *how* to make it better, I'll fix everything between us."

Nick gives a slight nod. "I don't envy you."

"No. I suppose you don't."

The floor creaks. Nick and I both look to see Megan standing just outside the room, the same familiar bathrobe wrapped tight around her. "We work with a *Nicolas*," she says.

6 YEARS AGO

Kendra checked the clock at the back of the classroom for the fifth time this period. *Fifteen more minutes,* she thought. It had been a long day —too long, and she wasn't looking forward to tomorrow. She'd been unable to think straight, not just during this class, but all day long.

"Guys, go ahead and pack up so we can all get out of here as soon as the bell rings," she said.

Her class didn't have to be told twice. Fifteen minutes of free time to sit and screw around—no work required—not a single one protested. They happily packed their books away and made themselves busy while Kendra sat at her desk, trying not to cry.

The computer monitor flashed a reminder.

Pick up Seth tomorrow at 8 AM

Kendra clicked the X in the corner to get rid of the notification. Seth would be home again. She'd been able to think of nothing else. Although she missed him more than anything, she wasn't sure if this would be a good reunion or not.

Kendra pulled up *Solitaire* until the bell finally rang. The kids filed out of the classroom, and she released a sigh of relief. *Alone at last,* she thought.

There were papers to grade and assignments to prepare for, but Kendra was having none of it. She hadn't been able to think all day. How was she supposed to concentrate on assignments? She waited long enough for the hallways to clear, then she grabbed her things and stepped out.

The first stop she wanted to make was Megan's classroom—on the other side of the school. Megan would distract her from her nerves, reassure her that it wasn't her fault her husband got sent to jail for a DUI, and maybe even take her out for an evening pedicure. She was the type of friend who always had your back and was exactly who Kendra needed to see right now.

Kendra nodded and waved to students on her way across campus, the stragglers who had nothing better to do than hang around in the hallways after school. *They're the ones who don't look forward to going home*, she thought. Normally she would be one of them, especially this last year. Her classroom was a second home—one she cherished, but today she'd been counting the minutes to escape.

Kendra came around a bend when someone knocked into her. She cried out in surprise, spilling her papers all over the hallway. She held a hand to her mouth to check for blood. There was none, but damn, that'd hurt.

"I'm so, so sorry," a man said, reaching to help her pick up. "God, I'm an idiot. Are you okay?"

For a moment, she thought he was a student. Then she saw the lanyard around his neck, the faculty badge hanging from the end of it, and the set of keys. Kendra stood. "It's okay. I was in too much of a hurry, wasn't paying attention."

"I'm so sorry," he said again, handing Kendra her papers.

"Are you new here?" she asked, mildly curious. He was young and good-looking—she was surprised he wasn't the topic of gossip in the teacher's lounge yet.

"Yes. I'm Nicolas, the new gym teacher. Well—temporarily, while Susan is on maternity leave."

"I'm Kendra McKnight. I teach English." She stuck out her hand to shake. "It's nice to meet you."

"Likewise."

There was a moment of silence, then Nicolas rushed to say, "Hey... can I buy you a drink? Or a cup of coffee, maybe? To say sorry for almost knocking you out?" He flushed, a little from embarrassment and a little because it had been a while since he'd asked a woman out.

It had been a while since Kendra had been asked out too, and she was tempted to take him up on the offer—*sorely* tempted. She hesitated before saying, "I'd love to but—I can't."

"Oh, of course. No problem, I totally—"

"But rain check?"

"Absolutely." He beamed. "I'll be around for a while still today—if you change your mind, that is."

As they parted ways, Kendra hoped Megan would still be in her classroom. She finally reached the door—it was locked. *Dammit, Megan, where are you?* Kendra thought. She pulled out her phone to call Megan—and was sent straight to voice mail.

Kendra thought about what she really wanted. She could go home, toss and turn all night, consumed with thoughts about Seth coming home tomorrow, she could continue trying to track Megan down—for God only knew how long, or she could go back and take Nicolas up on his offer. *It would be a friendly distraction*, she told herself—*nothing at all to do with how good-looking he is. Or how lonely I am...*

She felt ancient in his presence, so it wasn't really a lie. Nothing was going to happen, *especially* with a kid that much younger than her—one who could be one of her students. But she had an idea that taking him up on drinks would be a good way to ease some of the tension in her belly. She could get her mind off her estranged husband for a while, maybe—make a new friend while she was at it.

Finding this *Nicolas* that Kendra works with is going to be more of a challenge than it would seem. For one, unlike Nick, I haven't met him. And for two, she works at a high school—it's not like they let anyone waltz right in these days. Even if I check in at the front office, which I plan on doing, there better be a damned good reason for me being there. *And* even if there is, they'll call her.

I need a yearbook, and I need an excuse. Nick and Megan are kind enough to give me both, along with a change of clothes, since I'm still in my pajamas and bare feet. "That's him," Megan says, pointing to a picture of a man in an open yearbook. Beneath his picture is the name *Mr. Perez.*

My teeth automatically clamp down when I see him. *This* guy seems more like someone Kendra would be interested in. From his headshot, it's obvious he's good-looking.

"He's a gym teacher," she adds.

So she probably sees him a lot—bile rises in my throat just thinking about it. "Any ideas on how to get to him?"

"I'm not sure. Afternoons are best because the kids are rowdy after lunch. They aren't as focused in the afternoons, so our hands are usually a little fuller. *Kendra* will be busier—less likely to become aware of your presence."

"I can't wait until afternoon. I have to get to him first thing."

Megan frowns. "You can get into the gym and wait for him before class starts, but he might not be there. What if a kid comes in and sees you alone?"

"Let me worry about that. If you can get me into the gym, I think I'll have the rest covered."

"Are you worried about being alone with Nicolas?" Nick asks. "He might try to finish the job that Kendra started."

"Do you think he would try something at *school?*" Megan asks, horrified.

I think about what happened at Nick's office. I didn't think Kendra would try anything there, but she did. It doesn't seem likely that she or Nicolas would do something at the school but getting me alone in an empty gymnasium—they might. She seems to want to end me bad enough, at this point, I wouldn't put it past her.

Megan and Nick both look at me, waiting for an answer. "I don't know," I say. "But I have to speak with him. I have to try."

"I have a pistol—" Nick starts.

"No, thanks. I can't risk being caught with that on school property. It's all Kendra would need to frame me for something."

He grimaces. "You're absolutely sure you won't call the police and get them involved?"

"No. And I don't want you to either. Either of you." I glance between them. The looks on both their faces aren't quite what I'd like to see. These are good people who just want to do the right thing. Nothing I say will convince them that the police won't do any good. Not yet anyway. And if I start spewing talk about being stuck in a time—loop, they'll think I've got a screw loose.

"I need you to swear it," I say when neither speaks.

"But what if something happens?" Megan says.

Then I'll be reset, and none of this will matter anyway. "I need to get information from Nicolas. If the police come, I won't get that chance. *If* something happens, let it happen and call the police after."

Her eyes nearly bulge out of her skull. "You want me to *let* it happen?"

"That's right."

"I can't—"

"I need your help, Megan. Please."

She looks to her husband, who's still frowning, but nods. "We'll only call if you're hurt," he says.

"Okay," Megan finally gives in. Tears pool in her eyes like she's imagining Kendra, one of her dearest friends, going to prison or worse.

"Thank you both," I say, more relieved than either knows. "Now, any ideas on a reason for me to be there?" I'm not an educator, I have no kids, and I've never visited my wife at work before. I don't know what she would've told her coworkers about me, but I have a feeling just showing up out of the blue will be suspicious unless I go under the guise of someone else.

"Maybe claim to have a presentation for a class?" Nick says. He turns to Megan. "You can cover for him, right?"

She shakes her head. "Visitors like that need to be cleared in advance." She bites her lip. "I think you should just say it's your anniversary, and you want to surprise Kendra."

"You think that would work?"

"It's as good a reason as anything else. They'll check your ID, see that you're her husband."

"Will they tell her I'm there?"

"Maybe... but maybe not. The girls in the office like a good romantic gesture. They may not want to spoil her surprise."

"Wait a minute," Nick says. "If you're there early enough, is there really a need to check in at the office? Maybe he can just get inside the gym and not need to waste time doing things the 'right' way."

"I like the way you think," I say.

We both wait for Megan to speak. She's biting her lip again, wringing her hands together. "Security is really strict about strangers these days. If you're seen, it could get ugly. Are you sure you want to risk it?"

"If you think I have a shot, then yes. I'm—pressed for time."

Megan finally nods. "If we can get you there early enough, I think we'll be okay."

We scrap the plan about checking in at the office, about coming up with a lie for why I might be visiting my wife at work. Nick's right—there's no need to waste any more time than necessary. And if Nicolas isn't in the gym when I get there, I'll just have to wait for him until he shows up.

Later, Nick pulls me to the side when Megan is back upstairs. "I want you to have this. For just in case." He hands me a scalpel—identical to the one from his office. "I can't stand the thought of sending you to the wolves with no method of self-defense. And if you don't mind, don't tell Megan. She'd be furious."

I take it from him with a grateful nod. "I won't say a word." *This is going to be much more discreet than Kendra's knife.*

I can't believe how lucky I am that one of Kendra's best friends, and her husband, are so helpful. Megan and I were never on the closest terms. I met Nick maybe twice, and now I show up on their doorstep in the middle of the night with these accusations—and they're more than willing to help. I'm thankful my wife knows such good people because I'm not sure I would be so kind.

Their loyalty is a little questionable, all things considered, but it works out better for me. And I wonder if there's a reason that they believe me so easily. Despite what Kendra said, how she tried to convince me that Megan was *not* helping, I know better, and I know that deep down, Megan has to see evidence of Kendra's true nature for herself or even know the plan.

Maybe she's witnessed her lies firsthand, or perhaps violence. I wonder if there's ever been any parental complaints or other issues at school that Megan knows about but not me. Even Nick—*what if Kendra is cruel to our cat and he's seen signs of it?* My jaw tightens at the thought. I place a hand against my temple as my mind swims with dizziness. Whatever Kendra is doing or has done, it's been enough to garner me some much-needed help.

"Mind if I turn up the air?" I ask, moving the vent to blow more air directly at my face.

Megan looks at me, concerned. "Are you okay?"

"Fine, just a little tired." And saying the words, I realize just how tired I really am. It's more than merely *tired*, more like utterly drained. I feel like I'm in a car running on fumes, trying to drive up a hill, but can't find enough power to make it to the top. I keep pushing down on the accelerator, but there's no more fuel to feed the motor.

Megan reaches for the dial to crank up the air, giving me a doubtful look.

THE GYM HAS its own parking lot, and that's where Megan parks. I wait in the back, lying low across the seat in case anyone decides to peek through her windows. I bring my knees up to my chest, trying to fit my entire length in the tiny space and struggle not to moan against the discomfort. *It's only for a few minutes. Don't be a baby!*

The time on the dash reads 6:50. School doesn't start until eight, but Megan informed me that some teachers will show up an hour beforehand to prepare for the day. It's better for me—there are no kids around and hardly anyone at all. There's only one other car in the parking lot, and my hopes are set that it's Nicolas's.

As I wait for Megan to return from checking the gym door, my eyes grow heavier and heavier until I finally close them. *One Mississippi... two Mississippi... three Mississippi...* I count again to keep my mind occupied, but within a few seconds, I catch myself starting to drift. I sit up with a jolt, slapping myself across the cheek. *Don't fall asleep, goddammit!*

I can't risk a reset right now. I have to stay awake, focused, alert. Another glance at the clock reads 6:57. *God, how long is this going to take*—Megan's driver's door opens.

"Let's go," she says, peeking in at me.

Seconds later, we're on our way to the side entrance of the gymnasium. "Sorry, I had a minor distraction," Megan says. "You can go through the boy's side locker room. There's a teacher's office connected to it in back."

"Any sign of him?"

"None, but I didn't look inside. The door was locked." She pulls the door open for me now, keys dangling off the elastic band hanging from her wrist. "Good luck, Seth," she says.

I meet her worried eyes. "Thanks, Megan. You're a life-saver. I mean it."

"I wish I could do more."

"You can. Remember, no police."

She gives a firm nod. "I remember." Megan walks away while I slip into the boy's locker room.

I haven't been inside a gym locker room since I was a kid in high school, and being here brings back unpleasant memories. I'm not sure I've ever been in one this empty, even back then—it feels weird, almost *creepy*.

The lights are on a motion sensor, so as I move through, section after section turns on overhead. As I make my way to the back of the locker room, I start to hear what sounds like water. I pause to listen. Running water echoes through the room. *It's the showers!*

I inch my way to the edge of the lockers, finally seeing the showers to the left and the exit to the right. Megan said Nicolas's office would be through the exit, but the sound of the shower draws me in. *Why would there be a shower on when the door was locked?* Either it was left on from yesterday, or Nicolas is taking a morning shower.

The light above me goes dark again as I wait. When it does, I move into the tiled shower area, where each stall is blocked by a sheer hanging curtain. I look down at the wet floor, where a stream of water flows into a central drain.

My eyes widen when a long, low moan echoes around me. A woman's moan. One I would know anywhere.

I continue toward the stall with the running water, feeling like I've been gutted, feeling like my ears have been set on fire. Finally, I see two sets of feet beneath the curtain. I see their two bodies merged as one behind the sheer plastic. They're too busy to notice me watching them from three feet away.

Painted toenails twist to face a man's hairy feet. One of the polished feet lifts from the floor, the hairy feet rock forward as the man holds my wife up against the back wall of the tiled shower.

My hands start to shake. *What am I doing? Why am I watching this? I need to move, to get out of here, to stop this, to END this!* The image of my wife being screwed in the gym shower by another man—is seared into my brain for eternity. No matter how many deaths I endure, I'll never be rid of this.

I slip a hand into my pocket, pulling out the scalpel that Nick gave me for *just in case.* Without thinking, without even breathing, I pull the shower curtain aside with my free hand and slice the man's throat open, cutting as deep as I can get the tiny blade.

Blood sprays across Kendra's face, but she only smiles. "Took you long enough to show up."

I glare—at her and her sly smile, her swollen kissed lips, and wet, naked body still beneath the water. *She knew I would show up, knew I would find her this way—*

In one of Kendra's hands, she holds a gun. *They were—while she was holding a gun—in the shower!* She levels the pistol at me and without a word, pulls the trigger.

Being right has to be a worse hell than any kind of loop fate can stick me in. I'd rather face a thousand different loops than have to see Kendra—see *that* again. And yet, I know that's what I'm going to have to do.

How did she know? Megan? Did Megan betray me again? Or was it Nick? Either way, it doesn't matter now. I don't need to go to them again. I know where my road leads this time, and it will be useless to go to them.

As if on autopilot, I move through the motions one step at a time, doing exactly what I know will work to get me to where I need to be. I get the phone—*unlocked*—and the knife from under the pillow, avoid the cat, get down the stairs, get the keys—*both fobs,* don't slip and fall, don't crash. I navigate through the storm toward the school, ready to wait out the entire night in the parking lot.

Only when I'm across town and the streetlights finally shine through my windows do I realize I'm still in my pajamas and barefoot. *It's okay. No one's going to see me anyway. And if they do, who cares?* I may stick out like a sore thumb, but I'm not going to be out in the open long enough to care. *Besides, I'm going to be in a locker room. I'll fit right in—sort of.*

A RESET HAS DONE nothing to ease my exhaustion. It's worse now than when I had the dizzy spell in Megan's car, and I know there's nothing I can do to make it go away. Now that I'm away from Kendra with nothing to do, I'm *waiting* for hours, and just like the last time I did it, it's one of the hardest things I've ever had to do.

Sleep pulls at me with every breath I take. When I listen to the radio, all the talk is about *insomnia, sleep aids,* or *how to get a better night's sleep.* The games on Kendra's phone all have pop-up ads with pictures of couples bundled up under the covers, wrapped up together, and cozily sleeping.

Hours tick by on the clock, and somehow, someway, I manage to stay awake. I've slapped myself too many times to count—I know my face has to be red, but I don't bother looking in the mirror. I did what I had to do, and now the clock finally reads 6:57. *Time to move.*

I PLACE a hand on the door to the boy's gym locker room, expecting it to resist. I yank, and instead of it rattling against a lock, it pulls open free and clear. *Megan told me it was locked—*

I step inside, unhindered, the motion lights activating with my presence. As I move through the locker room, my mind reels. *Megan lied to me.* Why go through all that with me just to lie about the door being locked? Unless not going to seek her and Nick's help this time somehow changes the time line?

What else is going to be different? Is Kendra even here? My heart leaps in my chest at the possibility that she's not here betraying me at this moment. She could be stuck at home still or out looking for me. Maybe she spent the night at Megan's, trying to find me, and now has no idea where I might be.

As I approach the back of the locker room, the sound of water echoes around me, and then I hear it. That same long, low moan. And I know she *is* here. She is right on the other side of that tiled wall, getting her brains fucked out by some goddamn gym teacher.

My hand tightens around the handle of the knife—*Kendra's knife.* Instead of approaching them in the shower, I move back to the edge of a row of lockers, where I kneel out of sight and wait. One by one, the motion lights overhead turn back off. I wish I could block out the sound—I would do anything to not hear—but it's the only way I'll know when the coast is clear.

Whether Kendra decides to leave through to the gym or out the same door I came through, I'll know. She'll walk through here one way or another—and so will he. *Patience, Seth. Patience!*

Last time—I was unprepared. I wasn't ready to find Kendra like this, and—shame on me for letting it get the best of me. What did I really think was going to be happening? I *knew* she was cheating on me. Even if deep down I hoped I was wrong —I *knew* it.

The water turns off. I hear muffled voices, Kendra's giggle, then bare feet padding across the floor. They leave the shower area, setting off one of the motion lights.

"Meet me again tomorrow?" Nicolas says, voice drawing nearer.

"Tomorrow's Saturday." Kendra laughs. "But count me in for Monday." Her voice is fainter, moving in the opposite direction.

"Same time?" he calls.

"Yes!" she answers before the sound of footsteps against a gym floor.

"God, that was good," Nicolas says to himself, opening a locker.

"Was it?" I say, standing and moving around behind him.

He lets out a surprised yelp. "What are you—" He stops when he sees the knife I'm holding.

"I have a few questions for you, Nicolas."

"Nic—hang on. There's some kind of mistake here. I'm not Nicolas. I'm Mark."

"Mark?"

"Yeah. Now what the hell are you doing in here with that thing?"

I look at the knife that's gone limp in my grip. *Not Nicolas.* "What's your last name?"

"Why—"

"Just answer me." I hold the knife a little firmer.

"Perez."

Megan, that lying bitch! For all I know, police are going to show up any minute—or they would've last time. I take a steadying breath. "Is there anyone you work with named Nick or Nicolas?"

He hesitates, his eyes dart to the knife again.

"I'm not going to hurt anyone. This was just for personal protection, in case—you tried to attack me."

Mark laughs. "Attack you?" He runs a hand through his hair. "God, what a morning. Buddy, in case you don't know where we are..." He eyes my pajamas. "We're at a high school. The only one attacking anyone is you." He huffs, continuing.

"Look, you caught me at the right time. Kendra worked her magic. What can I say?" He grins. "Yeah, there's a Nicolas I work with. He's the other gym teacher, but he called in sick today."

"Do you share an office with him?"

"Yeah... it's through there," he says, pointing to the doorway leading to the gym.

At least Megan wasn't lying about everything. "Listen, Mark. This is important. Kendra—she tried to kill me."

His jaw drops. "Holy shit—"

"Did you have any idea? Did she say anything at all?"

"No way. We're not even that serious. She likes to have fun before school starts, that's all. She barely says five words the whole time." His look of worry grows. "I'm married, man. Please don't tell my wife about this—"

"So, you didn't know anything about her planning on killing anyone?"

"No! Why would I?"

I nod. "Thank you. You've been more helpful than you know."

"Who are you anyway? And can I get dressed now?"

"I'm her husband." I take a step toward him, slicing him across the throat before he can speak again.

Mark chokes on his own blood while I move to find Nicolas's address in their office.

CHAPTER
TWENTY-SEVEN

After searching through their shared office, I find a couple of documents that have Nicolas's name and address on them. With the information I need in hand, I clean the blood off myself and borrow a set of clothes from Mark's still-open locker. He won't miss them now, anyway.

When I leave the locker room, a few students linger in the halls. None seem to take notice of me, and I'm able to make my way back to the parking lot where the spaces are slowly starting to fill. In my truck, I take off as fast as I dare, not wanting to draw any attention. It won't be long before they find Mark's body, and I don't want to be around when it happens.

What will Kendra do when she finds out what I've done? Will she stay at work and pretend to wonder who the murderer is? Or will she leave and try to find me?

A few miles down the road, I pull over to enter Nicolas's address into the GPS. He doesn't live far from here. I rub my eyes, wishing again that I had my wallet so I could buy coffee, wishing I had the time to grab it and my phone from the kitchen instead of running for my life. Vision cleared, I shift into drive, thinking about what I'm going to say when I get there.

THERE ARE two cars parked in the driveway. I check the clock on the dash—7:37. *It's still early.* Whoever else is here might leave for work soon. *Or—they might've both called in sick to play hooky together.*

I wait. I can afford to wait a few minutes. Better *that* than have to figure out how to maneuver my way through this next hurdle.

There are a few options here. The document I grabbed from the office has Nicolas's phone number on it. I can call him and go from there.

Or I can just go up to the door and knock, just like I did with Megan and Nick. I can think of some excuse—some lie to get in, and if there is someone else home, I hope they're understanding. If they're not... I look at the back of my hands resting on the lower part of the steering wheel.

I killed a man less than an hour ago. They look like normal, average hands. You'd never know just by looking at them. *He fucked my wife in front of me—twice. How many other times did he do it that I don't know about?* He got more than he deserved. Next time—if there is a next time, I think I'm going to make him suffer a little more.

I still have the knife. At what cost? No—it won't come to that. I'm not going to be this person that Kendra's trying to make me be. I pull the knife from the inside pocket of my borrowed jacket and toss it on the floor of the back seat. It's staying here.

OVER AN HOUR PASSES, and it's now nearly nine. No one has left the house or even opened a door or window. I could be sitting here for nothing, no one even home despite the cars. Time to find out one way or another.

I look at Kendra's phone. When I called Megan and left that voice mail, she contacted Kendra. The chances are good that Nicolas will do the same, especially if he has her phone number saved to his contacts. *Looks like I'm doing this the old-fashioned way.*

I tuck the phone in my pocket and make my way to the front door. I ring the bell, hear it reverberate through the house. I wait a few seconds, listening for any sign of movement.

Nothing.

I ring it again and listen to the same sound echo through the house. I wait, but again there's nothing, no sign that anyone's home. I ring it again, this time pushing the bell button over and over in rapid succession.

Finally, there's movement—footsteps as the floor creaks inside. The door opens a crack, and a raspy voice says, "What the hell do you want?"

"I'm looking for Nicolas—" *What was his last name?* For the life of me, I can't remember. I try to bring up an image of the document in my brain, the one with his full name and phone number and address. It's in my pocket, but I can't pull it out now—

"He's sleeping."

"This is an emergency. Please, I'm so sorry to bother you,

but it's life or death."

The woman's eyebrows rise, intrigued. She looks me over before asking, "Who are you?"

"I'm Seth."

"Seth who?" She frowns.

"McKnight. I'm married to a colleague of his—Kendra McKnight."

The woman's frown deepens. "Wait here," she says before closing the door in my face.

Please don't let him call her! I wait impatiently, counting my Mississippis again. *I guess I'll find out soon enough if he does.* It's out of my hands now.

The knife is in the back seat... there's still time...

I imagine Kendra showing up and somehow ending my life again. I'll start over *again*, redo everything from the beginning. How many times is it going to continue to happen? I swore there'd be no more Mr. Nice Guy—I look back at the truck, torn.

No. I'm not going to do this!

I hear the sound of a car approaching. My hands start to sweat. I look down the road, trying to see, and back at my truck. I don't see a car, but the sound is growing closer.

I take a step forward.

The door behind me opens again. "He's up," the woman says.

I spin back around and enter the house, my heart racing.

"Hey, everything okay?" she asks, eyeing me closely. It's clear she's hesitant to let me in their home.

"No," I say. "It's an emergency, remember?"

"Right. Well, you can wait here." She points to the couch in the living room. "Nicolas will be out in a minute."

I take a seat, fighting to calm my heart rate and not pass out into the cushions as I wait for him.

Footsteps come from down the hall. I sit up a little straighter, not sure if I should stand—when a young man greets me. "Hi," he says. "Can I help you?"

I bite my lip to keep from grimacing. *This is just a kid!* "Hi, um—" I look around the house, trying to get any kind of hint that this is the man I'm looking for. "Are you Nicolas?"

"That's right."

"I'm sorry, I think there's a mistake. I'm looking for one of the gym teachers at the high school."

He smiles. "I get that all the time. I know I'm young—but I'm twenty-eight, and yes, I'm one of the teachers. My mom said you know Kendra?"

There is no way in hell that's this guy's age. He looks more like eighteen or twenty—maybe. "I'm her husband. She—" I clear my throat, trying to think of the best way to put it. "She's having an affair with Mark."

Nicolas frowns, looking apologetic. "I'm aware of that. I mean—I didn't know she was married, only that there was something going on with Mark."

"And are you—close to her too?"

He holds up his palms in front of himself. "No, sir. She's a little too old for my taste." He blushes. "And besides, I don't like to mix work relationships like that. Too messy—I learned that the hard way."

I might be a fool, but I believe this guy. Something about him doesn't strike me as the type to mess around with an older woman that he works with. Not that Kendra is that old—she's only thirty-five. But I smile anyway, picturing the look on her face at being called *old* by a twentysomething guy.

Nicolas starts to relax when he sees my smile. He lowers his hands and sits next to me on the couch. "You believe me?" he asks.

"Yes. And I appreciate your honesty. But there's more I need to know."

He nods. "I'll help if I can."

"Kendra—tried to kill me last night."

At this, Nicolas's whole upper body flushes. He backs away from me as far as the couch will allow. "Are—are you okay?" he asks.

"I'm okay... but I need to know if you know anything about it. If she said anything to you at all?"

"No! No, of course not. And if she did—that's insane to even think about!"

"You never overheard her saying anything to Mark? No plot...?"

"No. I swear it, and like I said—if I did, I would've told someone."

The veins in my neck are starting to pop out with the effort I'm putting into clenching my jaw shut. My teeth grind back and forth as I think about what he's telling me. I watch Nicolas— and he watches me, wringing his hands together while he does.

The problem is—I believe him. He seems like a good kid. His mom—wherever she went off to, seems like a decent enough person, too. Decent people don't conspire to murder other people. This kid doesn't know anything about it. But where does that leave me?

"There's nothing else you can tell me?" I say, trying one last time to get any piece of information.

Nicolas plays with his lips, pinching them with his fingers as he thinks. "All I know is that I've seen her around before and after school. Sometimes they ask to speak privately in our office—and I know they're not talking." He flushes, continuing. "I try not to be around when that's going on. I'm sorry I can't be more helpful."

"When I got away from her last night, she asked me if Nick told me. Other than yourself... do you have any idea who Nick might be?"

He holds a hand to his chest. "No one calls me that. You would think they might, but no. I go by Nicolas, and I correct anyone who gets it wrong. If Kendra was talking about a 'Nick' she wasn't talking about me."

"So, no idea who she *was* talking about then?"

Nicolas shakes his head. "No. I mean, there might be another teacher at the high school, but none that I'm familiar with."

"You wouldn't happen to have a yearbook I can borrow?"

He brightens. "That, I do have. I'll grab it." He stands and leaves the room. From across the house, he shuffles through a closet, calling, "Mom, what'd you do with last year's yearbook?"

She yells something to him from the back of the house. It does the trick. A few moments later, Nicolas returns with a yearbook in hand. "Here you go. You can take as long as you need to look over it."

I take it from him. "Thanks, man. I appreciate you trying to help, and I'm sorry for dragging you into my mess of a marriage."

"Hey, it's no problem. And you're not the one dragging me into it. Kendra should've been more discreet. It's almost like she was screaming, 'look at me.' I'm surprised they haven't got caught by anyone else—they both could get fired for what they..."

He trails off as I start to flip through the yearbook pages, realizing I don't want to hear any more details about my wife and her lover, especially ones that aren't going to help me figure anything out.

"I'll leave you to it," he says, walking back down the hall.

I find the page that Megan showed me earlier, with the picture of Mark that she tried to play off as Nicolas. Beneath the photo reads the same *Mr. Perez*. Other pages show other pictures of teachers with students, but none have the teacher's first name, until I hit the back of the book, where there's a faculty page.

Why didn't I think of this before? Megan—my fingers tighten around a page, crumpling it in my grip as I think about all the lies. It would seem she and my wife are a perfect match.

On the faculty page, I scan everyone's face and name, looking for anyone who might look familiar to me, or anyone named *Nick*. Even another Nicolas or Nicolai. Hell, I'd settle for a close-sounding name like Mick.

But there's nothing here. None who fit the bill. Not a single other faculty member named anything that could be considered relatively close to what I need. I'm reset again, without dying this time, and now, I don't know where to start or where to go.

I close the yearbook, leaving it on the couch, and make my way out the front door without bothering to say goodbye to Nicolas or his mom.

CHAPTER
TWENTY-NINE

The streets are still wet from last night's storm. Leaves cover the roads and sidewalks. Pumpkins still out from Halloween are starting to collapse in on themselves, soggy from all the rain.

I drive through town aimlessly. With no more clues, no more hints, all the *lies*—what can I do? Never in my life have things felt so hopeless, not even as a kid when it seemed like the world might end if things went wrong. In this case—my world really *is* ending.

As I navigate, I start to think more about the loop itself. *What if I'm assuming things that aren't true?* I'm assuming I can't fall asleep, but what if I'm wrong and I can? Just thinking about sleep makes my eyes water.

And with all these resets—I've been thinking about having a limit, a maximum number of lives before the game is over and the credits roll. What if there is *no* max number? Or time limit for each *round*—so to speak? And what's more, why bother getting out of this loop at all? If I can avoid Kendra for the rest of my life, why not just live like normal until I'm eighty or ninety, die, then reset and turn into a thirty-eight-year-old again?

I could try it. I could leave, start a life somewhere else, try to make it work. *How long until she finds me, and I wake up in that bed next to her again?*

As screwed up as it sounds, part of me wants it. Kendra is my other half—how can I just leave without knowing why? How can I just give up without solving this? She's my *wife*. We've been married for nearly a decade—that's a damned accomplishment. Now all of a sudden, she's doing everything she can to murder me... and I'm thinking about just *leaving*?

My foot presses harder on the accelerator. Driving faster than necessary always helps ease a little tension, and it works now too. The sound of the truck's exhaust grows louder as the engine comes to life beneath the hood.

Rain starts to patter against my windshield. *What's it going to be, Seth?* Nowhere to go now... but home.

What if I can't figure this out? A ball of doubt is growing in the pit of my stomach, weighing me down. I'm starting to think I'm not going to be able to do this. Even if I figure out why Kendra wants me dead—so what? What's that going to do? It solves nothing. And even if it did end the loop, I can't believe a damn word out of her mouth.

I'm starting to think I should just—*let it go.* So what if she keeps killing me? Maybe it won't be *so* bad. I'll get used to it... *maybe.* I think about the lingering pain that each stab brings, each slice across my flesh, each bullet through my body...

My eyes close as I release a yawn so deep it hurts. My tires whine against the grooves in the middle of the road. I force my eyelids back open, jerking the steering wheel to get back in my lane.

I won't get used to the tiredness—the pure exhaustion. I can't get used to it because it's only getting worse. Even when I reset, it's like I haven't slept at all in who knows how long. And if I don't find an end to this, let it go on forever, I think I'll get to the point where I can't wake up at all. *That* will be my true death, *or that'll be when I truly wish for it.*

Something tells me fate hates my guts at the moment. If it didn't, why else would this be happening to me? No matter what I want, I don't think fate will just stand back and let me do nothing. One way or another, I'm going to have to stand my ground or keep running.

I turn the truck down the road that was blocked by a fallen tree last night. The tree is cleared now, pieces of leftover bark in the road the only sign that there's been anything amiss. Hopefully, the power is back on now too.

My mind is so fuzzy it's starting to be a challenge to keep my thoughts straight. I have the wipers on faster than they need to be, because any buildup of rain blocks the vision from my tired eyes. I can't concentrate like I normally can. *What I would give for just a catnap!*

Maybe I'm wrong, I remind myself. Sleep could not be a problem at all, and I'm just making it one. What if fate doesn't care about me sleeping and refueling? My stomach growls, reminding me I need to eat too.

Suddenly, I'm glad I made the choice to go home.

There's no place like home, isn't that right, Dorothy?

That's right, Toto.

My mouth salivates, thinking about all the food in the pantry cupboard, waiting to go right down my throat. My eyes grow heavy thinking about the soft couch cushions calling my name. I won't sleep upstairs, but I'm going to give it a go on the couch. If I wake up back in my bed, at least I'll know one way or another.

Kendra should be at school still—for how long, there's no way to know.

I don't slow the truck until I finally reach the end of our

driveway. I hit the remote for the garage door, holding my breath as it opens.

The car is gone. No Kendra. I can almost cry—but I'm too tired and too hungry.

I make my way into the house, grabbing food just like I imagined doing. The fridge is full of leftover dinner, and the pantry has my favorite snacks. I eat and eat and eat some more, until my stomach is more than full. I open a bottle of cold water from the fridge and chug it down, not caring when it spills onto my shirt. *Who knows when I'll get to eat or drink again?*

When I'm finally done, finally satisfied, I move to the living room. The couch is so beautiful with its dark-brown leather, so soft, so smooth. I rub my hand across the armrest, coaxing it to let me sleep on it *just for a little while.* I look around the room, another quick glance. *No sign of her.*

With a sigh, I lie down. Within two seconds, I'm asleep.

CHAPTER THIRTY

5 YEARS AGO

K endra silenced her phone for the third time that evening. "Sorry, where were we?" she said, tucking it back into her purse.

Her date cleared his throat. "You know... you could just turn it off—if there's someone who won't stop bugging you."

"I probably should, but I'm sure that would just make him angrier." She smiled at the man across from her. "I'm not hungry anymore. You wanna get out of here?"

He did, and they did.

It was the middle of the night by the time she got home. Seth was waiting up for her with the downstairs light on. Kendra started when she saw him sitting there with a beer in hand, reclined back on the couch, looking haggard.

She didn't want to see him this way—lower than she'd ever known him. She started to walk past him to the stairs.

"Where were you?" he asked.

"I told you before—a faculty dinner."

"Don't bullshit me, Kendra." He pushed the couch recliner in, stood, and came toward her.

"I don't want to argue," she said, turning away. It was like this almost every day since he'd come home from prison—whether she came home late or not, and she'd had enough.

Seth grabbed hold of her wrist to stop her. "I don't want to keep sitting here night after night, waiting for you to come home, wondering *if* you'll come home—and all the while you're out there fucking someone else."

"Well, maybe if you had a job, you wouldn't need to sit here and wait for me." Kendra yanked her hand away from him. She looked at the beer in his other hand. "Don't you think you've had enough?"

"I'm not a goddamn drunk, and you know it. And you know I've been trying, too. No one wants to hire an ex-con. And if they do hire me, they fire me for nothing."

"You had a DUI. You're not a murderer."

"They don't care. It's all the same to them."

Kendra clamped her jaw shut before she said something she'd regret. *Poor me is all it ever is*, she thought. She was being cruel to him, maybe, but she was also fed up.

"I'm beat," she said, starting to leave again.

"Me not having a job has nothing to do with what you're doing," Seth said.

Kendra ignored him. She dropped her purse off and went upstairs.

THE NEXT MONTH, Kendra had another *faculty dinner* to attend. Her phone went off religiously—Seth again, no doubt calling to find out where she was. He called her like clockwork when she wasn't home by a certain time. Kendra silenced her phone, tucked it back into her purse, and smiled up at her date.

"IT'S GETTING LATE," she said.

"Do you... want to get out of here?"

She grinned. "I'd love to."

He drove them to his place. Inside, they were too busy *not talking* in the bedroom to notice Seth sneaking in through the front door. Once inside, he found them easily enough. He stood, watching another man love his wife. As he did, something inside him shriveled up and died.

"Kendra," he said.

Shocked, her date jumped back from her, and when he turned to see Seth standing in his bedroom, he yelled, "Who the hell are you? Get out!"

Kendra stared at Seth, unable to believe he had found her and was actually here. "Go home, Seth."

Her date turned to her. "You know this asshole?"

"This asshole is her husband," Seth said.

He charged at the man, not thinking, only feeling the rage that threatened to burn him alive. He attacked with full force, each blow against the stranger a balm. Only when the stranger was on the floor bleeding, begging for mercy, did he stop.

Seth held an arm out toward Kendra. "Come on. We're going home."

She went with him.

BEFORE THEY WALKED through the front door, Seth pulled Kendra to him. "I don't want to lose you," he said.

"You won't."

"Stop this bullshit then. Stop doing this to me."

"You know... I kind of liked seeing you get angry." She gave him that look that he loved—the one she hadn't shown him in so long.

Seth held her around her waist. "I'm serious. Don't do this to me anymore."

She said nothing.

He kissed her, then he took her upstairs.

CHAPTER
THIRTY-ONE

I open my eyes—then close them. I wait on the verge of tears. I open them again—back in bed. Kendra is next to me. The storm is raging outside, everything is reset.

And I'm still tired.

I grip the sheets in my fists, wanting to scream. Can a person lose their sanity from lack of sleep? I'm not sure, but I'm starting to think it's a possibility.

I feel so *angry*—more now than when this first happened. Finding out that I can't go to sleep is somehow worse than death itself. Is this what insomniacs feel like? Is this how they live every day of their lives? Why isn't this talked about more? How do—

Wait a minute.

I look back at Kendra huddled beneath the blankets. I didn't *think* she was home... but what if she was? What if she killed me in my sleep? If *that* reset me, I would never know it. I could've been asleep for hours—

Then why don't I feel rested?

Maybe I *did* feel rested until she reset me again.

Does that really make sense?

Does any of this make sense? I'm talking to myself—

"Seth?"

I sigh. "I'm awake."

"What's wrong?"

"Can't sleep."

She sits up to look at me. "Me either," she says.

"Hey—" I want to ask her, not like the man she's trying to kill, but like her *husband*. I long to have a conversation like we used to, like *normal* before all this—when every word out of her mouth wasn't a lie—she would tell me things I could actually believe.

I miss her. The feeling hits hard, right in the middle of my chest. I take a deep breath, ready to say something lame like maybe *I love you...* only—I can't. My lungs are tight. I can barely get air in.

I gasp, trying to get more oxygen, but there's something blocking them. I'm getting hot, breaking out in a sweat with nerves and heat. *Why can't I breathe?*

Kendra comes closer, a shocked expression on her face. Whatever this is—it's not her doing. "Seth, what's happening?" she asks, and from her voice, she actually *sounds* concerned.

Interesting, all things considered.

"I can't—" I gasp and suddenly my left shoulder feels like it's being squeezed in a vise. The pain intensifies, moving down the entire length of my arm. I grip it with my right hand, trying to give counterpressure.

No, this can't be happening! I'm too young—

Kendra realizes what's happening almost as soon as I do. "You're having a heart attack," she says.

I stare up at her, knowing she won't do a damned thing about it.

She worries her lip between her teeth, watching me struggle to breathe.

Nausea rises in my throat. I start to fight it down, but then smile, thinking about the look on her face if I barfed all over her.

Kendra places a soft hand gently against my chest. She leaves it there, waiting, feeling my heart stop beneath her palm. Our eyes stay connected until the life finally leaves my body.

CHAPTER THIRTY-TWO

I'm somewhat young still, I'm healthy, or at least—I think I am. I've never had any health problems. So why did I just have a heart attack? Was it from the lack of sleep and the stress? Is that possible?

Whatever the reason, it doesn't really matter. Now that I've had one, I'm more likely to have another. *Great.* Just what I need—*another* way to die.

There's one thing left for me to try, though, one final test to see if I'm right about Kendra killing me in my sleep. Before I waste any more time thinking about what just happened, I force myself to get up and go through the motions again. I do everything I need to do to get out of the house.

I could stay home, hide in the barn... but I have to get the truck out of the driveway. If I don't move it, Kendra will never leave. She'll know I'm still here. She'll search for me until she finds me, and that won't do. So, I get in the truck and drive across town to the high school.

There are probably tons of places that would be fine to stay, but I parked here before, and she never showed. No one did. I was safe the entire night with no one around to bug me, and I have my hopes up that it'll be safe again.

The perfect spot around the back of the building glows beneath a streetlight, waiting for me. My spine tingles as I think about lying down across the back seat, stretching my back, and embracing the darkness.

I park the truck, take out Kendra's phone, and set an alarm. *Wouldn't want to oversleep.* I smile to myself. *That would be such a nice way to wake up—a security guard banging against the window, waking me when he hears my snoring from across the parking lot.*

After adjusting the front seats forward to give myself more room in the back, I move into the back seat. I lie down, make myself as comfortable as possible, and still full of hope, I close my eyes.

CHAPTER
THIRTY-THREE

I open my eyes... blink... and sigh. I clench them closed again. *No, no, no!*

It didn't work. I'm back in bed, next to Kendra, *reset.* *Why? Why does this have to be happening?* My last hope has failed, and I'm right back to where I started.

I leave my eyes closed, and soon, I start to drift. *It's fine. I'll just keep sleeping and resetting, sleeping and resetting. I don't need to go anywhere or do anything.*

Only—I don't fall asleep. Kendra makes a sound next to me, shifting on the bed. Thunder rolls, making the window rattle. I move over onto my side.

I could get up...

To do what? To go where?

I stay where I am and wait. *Maybe I can fall back asleep before she—*

Too late. Kendra is already climbing over me with the knife in hand.

CHAPTER
THIRTY-FOUR

I'm awake, but I keep my eyes closed, trying to go back to sleep. *This is a nightmare—a bad dream. I can just go back to sleep.* I repeat the lie.

And it will keep happening over and over for eternity... I'll have to feel that knife's edge so many times it'll be like a second skin to me.

I don't care. I'm staying. I'm going to hit the hay. I'm not putting in any more effort toward something that's never going to happen. I'll never solve this, never figure it out. Kendra can kill me over and over if that's what she wants.

It's too bad she doesn't know what I'm going through. I'm sure she would *love* this. She would cherish the thought of killing me a hundred times over and over. The way her face would light up—

Hang on—

She would be happy. More than happy—she would be *ecstatic.*

I said it before—that maybe I'm going about this all wrong... and maybe I *still* am. Nicolas said something about Kendra that comes back to me.

It's almost like she's screaming 'look at me.'

I tried to ignore him, to block out any details of her betrayal, but what if he was onto something? Kendra was looking for attention. She wanted me to notice her. What if this isn't about running away and surviving? What if it's about making her happy? What if the whole point of this is to save my marriage?

They say the universe works in mysterious ways... maybe this is one of them. Maybe I've been too frightened and too blind to see what's right in front of me. And now that I'm so tired I can't think straight, I'm finally seeing things from another angle. My wife wants me to see her. She wants me to notice and probably to care enough to do something about it.

I finally open my eyes. Kendra is already above me, looking down at my face. "I see you," I say, watching her closely.

"I see you too, Seth."

We lock gazes, and something seems to pass unspoken between us. Her features are full of anger and hate, but her eyes—behind them there's something else. Longing, loneliness, maybe even hurt.

"It's okay," I whisper, barely audible against the sound of thunder.

"You don't mind?" she asks, tilting her head. Slightly amused.

"Well, I prefer not to die. But I forgive you. Wife."

Her chin wobbles as she tries to hold back tears. She opens her mouth to speak, to say something. *It's on the tip of her tongue.* But she closes back up.

Instead of confessing some deep, dark emotion, some terrible secret to why she has to do this, she brings up the knife and gets it over with.

CHAPTER THIRTY-FIVE

Kendra stared at herself in her car's visor mirror, twisting her head this way and that. She opened the tube of lipstick, applied a fresh layer, then smiled in the mirror to make sure she didn't get any on her teeth. *Everything looks straight, nothing sagging—too much*, she thought, ignoring the first couple of wrinkles making their appearance. She got out of the car and made her way inside the restaurant.

Inside, the hostess looked past her, expecting to see someone with her. "Just one tonight?" she asked with a smile.

"No, we have reservations for two under McKnight."

She looked through the tablet at the podium, but after a moment of searching and still not finding the name, she frowned. "What time was the reservation for?"

"It was for six thirty. I know I'm a few minutes early…"

The hostess continued to search; she whispered something to another hostess next to her. Finally, she shook her head. "I'm sorry, I don't see a reservation for tonight. I might be able to squeeze you in if you don't mind waiting."

"I don't understand. There's definitely a reservation. Try the spelling M-c-K-n-i-g-h-t."

She looked again. "I'm sorry, ma'am. Did you want to wait? It looks like there's about to be a table ready. It should be available within a few minutes."

"Fine," Kendra said. She moved to the waiting area, embarrassed and upset. *If Seth wasn't on his way right now* —she thought. She brought out her phone to text him.

You made reservations, right? They couldn't find our name.

She waited. Fifteen minutes later, a server led her to a table in the corner near a cozy fireplace. He left her with a menu, but the first thing she did was text Seth again.

Just got seated. Where are you?

Kendra ordered a drink and waited. More time passed. The waiter came, delivered the wine, and she waited some more. She sent another text to Seth.

Hello? Earth to Seth!

She sipped her glass of wine, discreetly checking the time. *Thirty minutes late... where the hell are you, Seth?* she thought. She wasn't used to sitting alone at a restaurant and it seemed like all eyes kept drifting her way, wondering who the idiot standing her up was. *Just my husband!* she thought. She sent another text.

Where are you?

She didn't know what to do with her hands—thought it was awkward to sit there on her phone, flipping through social media or playing games, but probably more awkward if she didn't. It only took so long to check the menu. She didn't want to sit there staring into space while Seth took his sweet time meeting her. He still hadn't answered a single message.

She sent him a text for the fifth time.

Where Are You???????

Kendra noticed that the message bubble that was supposed to be blue—sent as green. They all had. When that happened, it could mean a few different things, but usually included no cell service. *It's okay,* she thought. *He's on his way here, passing through the no-cell zone.* There was a stretch of highway where the trees were too thick. That was most likely where he was.

She only lasted sixty seconds before she texted again.

Are you really doing this to me today?

Kendra made herself look busy on her phone, declining a refill when the server came back to offer more wine. Time passed with still no answer from Seth. She checked the clock again, so angry she was shaking. *Over an hour. How long are you going to keep waiting?* she thought.

She decided to give it one last chance—that was it. If he didn't answer, she was leaving. Instead of texting, this time she called. It rang once—she was relieved he at least hadn't turned the phone off—it rang twice, three times. Just as she was about to end the call, he answered.

"Hey."

"Where are you?" she asked, controlling her temper. She'd rip him a new one at home, but for now, others were probably listening in on her conversation, and she didn't want to be even more embarrassed.

"I'm on my way home."

"*Why?*" It came out as a surprised shout, drawing all eyes her way. She tucked her head down. "I've been trying to get a hold of you," she hissed.

"Sorry. I left my phone in my truck for the interview."

"Wasn't that this morning?"

Kendra could hear the grin in his voice as he said, "Yeah, and I got the job! They wanted me to do a trial run today—see what I'm—"

She hung up, trembling.

Seth tried to call back—she declined his call and turned off her phone. After settling the bill, she left.

Angry tears broke through the well-constructed dam. Kendra sat in her car, staring at herself through the visor mirror once again. "Happy anniversary," she said. He pulled the same thing on their wedding day—it seemed a fitting anniversary present. *When is it going to be enough?* she thought.

She had no answer. She wondered if she was overreacting. Seth couldn't be the first man in the world to do this to his wife. And he'd gotten the job... it hurt—yes—but should she keep stoking the fire or let it burn out? It used to be such a clear-cut answer. And now—

I see you, Kendra. If I ever saw anyone, it's you. I'm going to fix this. I'm going to set things right between us. *And when I do, this damned loop will be over.*

My heartbeat jumps at the thought. *Could this really be the answer I've been looking for? The "why" I've been trying to figure out?*

Before I lose my chance, I slip beneath Kendra's pillow to grab the knife and phone, just like normal. I've almost got it down to a science now and know when I still have an opening and when time is too far gone to even bother trying. Luckily, this time is easy enough.

Kendra starts to complain when I lift up her pillow, but quiets when she sees the knife. "It's okay," I say, smiling. "I'm not mad."

Her face drops into that cold, blank stare that I despise. "What are you going to do?" she asks.

I pull the top sheet from the bed and use the knife to rip it down the middle. "Put your arms up against the headboard."

For a moment, she stares at me, unmoving, and I think she's not going to do as I asked. As I step closer though, she complies without complaining. I grip one of the sections of the sheet and move over to her side of the bed. Bunching it up in a flat line like a rope, I use it to tie one of her arms through a loop in the headboard.

When she's secure, I tie her other hand with the other section of the sheet and stand back to look at my handiwork.

"Satisfied?" she asks.

"I sure am. Now I know you're not going to sneak up on me and stab me to death while I make you breakfast." I lean over to kiss her forehead, and as I do, she pushes her head back into the headboard, trying to get as far away as possible. I pretend to ignore it. *It's fine. Everything is fine.*

"Well, it's the middle of the night... too early for food, but maybe not for a movie?" I raise my eyebrows in question. "What do you think?"

"What the hell game are you playing at, Seth? Untie me or kill me. Whatever you're going to do—get it over with."

"I'm not going to hurt a hair on your head. Don't you ever say that!"

She eyes the knife that's resting at the foot of the bed.

"*You* had that. Not me."

"You have it now, don't you?"

"Fine." I take the knife, open the bedroom door, and set it out in the hallway, making sure I won't step on it if I need to leave the room. I turn back to her with a smile. "Do you feel safer now?"

Her eyes narrow like she's trying to solve a riddle. She doesn't trust me, doesn't believe that I'm trying to make things right instead of worse. I don't know how she could ever think I would hurt her. I physically *can't*—not that I would ever want to.

Even with Kendra murdering me over and over, I have no desire to harm her. I should've never even tried with her wrist —it was pointless. I'm too afraid now that it would be permanent, and I'd lose her forever. I just need her to understand how much she means to me.

Kendra doesn't answer me, so I reach over to turn on her bedside lamp—and remember the power's out. "Sorry, looks like no TV after all," I sigh. "We could talk?"

"Go to hell."

"Would it kill you to tell me the truth? Why do you want me dead so bad, Kendra?"

She turns her head, staying silent.

"I just don't get it," I say. "What are you so afraid of saying? You're going to kill me! Why on earth can't you just tell me why?"

Kendra remains silent, refusing to give me the answer I long to hear. I can only hope I've figured it out now, and not just that—that I'm actually going about fixing things between us and not driving the wedge further in.

I bring out Kendra's phone and open her games folder. I browse through the choices she already has downloaded and stop when I land on *Monopoly*. *This will keep us busy for a while.* I set up the game, choosing a piece for each of us—Kendra as the car and me as the dog.

I climb across her legs and position myself next to her on the bed so that we can both see the screen. "What are you doing?" she asks.

"We're playing *Monopoly*." I flick my finger across the screen to roll the dice. The dog moves across the board, and when my turn ends, I say, "Your turn."

Kendra stares at me.

"Oh, right. Sorry." She's tied up, so I have to roll for her. I flick my finger across the screen again, and this time her car moves around the board. "Do you want to buy it?" I ask when she lands on one of the railroads.

She shakes her head, and I flick my finger across the

screen again to start my turn. My heart hammers in my chest being this close to her. *Alive. And she's starting to engage. This is going to work!*

We keep playing the game, and slowly, Kendra thaws out of her ice shield. She yells at me when I charge her rent on my hotels, she laughs when I land on her Boardwalk and Park Place, and she insists on a rematch when I kick her ass. I grin at her, wishing I could trust her enough to untie her hands. Her fingers have to be going numb by now. I look at them—*no. Still too soon.*

I bring up another round on her phone, daring to let myself hope.

A few hours pass without either of us noticing. It's almost a miracle in itself. When the storm stops and rays of sun start to come up through the clouds, Kendra yawns. "We've been playing this for hours. I'm starving."

"Me too. I'll fix us something." I set her phone on my nightstand and move to get off the bed.

"Wait a minute." She nods toward her hands. "Do you think you can untie me?"

"Sorry. We're still not on that level yet."

"How am I supposed to eat?" Her eyebrows lift and she looks at me expectantly.

"We'll worry about that when the time comes. For now, I'm going to leave you for a few minutes. Now that it's not so dark, I can actually see where I'm going." I head to the door in a better mood than when I woke up. Spending time together has been good for us, even if we've just been playing a game.

The last time we stayed up playing *Monopoly* was—I don't even remember when. Probably years ago, maybe before we were even married. This was good.

I smile at Kendra before I leave the room. She doesn't

smile back, but she doesn't grimace either. "I'll be right back. I promise I'm not going to leave you here all day."

She nods.

DOWNSTAIRS, I check the light switch at the bottom of the stairs, and it comes on. The power is back. *Things are looking up already.* I move to the kitchen and crack some eggs in a pan. Bacon in the microwave, hash browns in the air fryer, sliced strawberries on the side, and soon, I have a tray filled with Kendra's favorite breakfast.

I add an extra plate for myself, my mouth watering just looking at the meal I've created. I'm damned proud of myself. I don't normally cook, but I figured out how to do all this! I'm sure Kendra is expecting me to come back with a bowl of cereal—well, this will show her.

I eye the jug of orange juice in the fridge. *Better not.* Drinks will have to wait because I'm not risking a spill.

With the tray in hand, I start back up the stairs, pleased with myself. All those times I died—for what? I still don't really *know*, but my point is—I could've stayed and tried instead of running. Running is something I've done a lot in our life together, but no more.

And putting in the one-on-one time is actually a nice change. And fun! So much that I almost feel like a kid again. Kicking her ass in *Monopoly*—I grin just thinking about it. *I hope she's up for another round or maybe another game.*

Using my back, I nudge the door open, still smiling. "Your feast awaits," I say, turning to face Kendra.

"Oh, Seth, you shouldn't have."

"So it would seem."

Kendra is no longer tied to the headboard. She's holding a gun—pointed straight at me. I gulp, recognizing the gun—same gun—she had in the back of the car—and in the shower. *She must've been keeping it up here as a backup in case the knife didn't work.*

"Set the tray on the dresser."

I do as she asks, then turn back to face her, hoping the pleading look on my face will appeal to her blackened heart.

"You don't have to do this. I thought we've been moving forward, putting all this behind us?"

"By playing a board game?" she says, incredulous.

"By spending time together even after I knew what you wanted to do. I still love you, Kendra, don't you see?"

"No. I don't see." She pulls the trigger.

I*t's okay.* I'll just... try again. I need to find the gun and tie a better knot around her wrists—or maybe... I don't need to tie one at all if I find all her secret weapons. She won't have anything else to kill me with, and maybe it will warm her to me more.

First things first.

Trying to hang on to that thread of confidence that Kendra just shot at, I force myself to get up and get the knife and phone from beneath her pillow. From there, I don't tie her up, but I do finally think to use the light on her phone to search the room. *I wish I would've thought of it sooner...*

"Hey, would you mind telling me where the gun is, dear?" I ask, shuffling through our dresser drawers.

"What gun?"

"The one you're trying to hide from me." I turn back around to face her. "Don't bother lying about it. I already know you have one in here somewhere, just like I knew about the knife."

She shrugs. "I don't know what you're talking about."

This isn't going to do any good. She's never going to give up the gun, just like she never gave up the knife. I'm either going to have to keep dying over and over just trying to find it, or I'm going to have to keep her in my sights at all times.

I take a steadying breath, setting the phone on the dresser since I don't have pockets. "Fine. It's okay." I take a step toward her. "I think we started on the wrong foot. Let's just relax. Can I draw you a bath?"

"A *bath*?" Her eyebrows shoot up.

"Yeah, why not?"

"It's still the middle of the night, for one."

"Exactly. Nice warm water, some bubbles and bath salts—a perfect way to relax and get back to sleep." I reach for her hand.

She pulls back. "I don't want to take a bath."

"Give me your hand."

"No. I don't want to."

I grab her arm and pull, forcing her to come with me. She stumbles in the dark and I have to pull her up more than once. In the bathroom, Kendra puts the toilet seat lid down to sit and wait for her bath.

I turn the faucet, the water comes rushing out in a burst, then just as fast, it slows to a drip. *Shit!* I look at Kendra, waiting with her arms crossed, *glaring* at me. "The power's out." *How the hell did I forget there's no water with no electricity?*

"It's fine. I didn't want a bath anyway—like I tried to tell you."

"I'm sorry. I was just trying to do something nice for you."

"... that I didn't want." Her attitude isn't helping anything, and she knows it. She wants to see me squirm.

"I'll read to you if you'd like that?" I offer, trying not to sound irritated. Kendra used to beg me to read chapters at a time to her out of whatever book she was reading while we lay in bed. She said she loved the sound of my voice and the feel of my chest thrumming against her ear when I spoke. I always hated to do it, hated her cheesy romance stories, and hated reading out loud like I was in school again. I put her off every time she asked until finally she stopped asking.

Kendra seems surprised by my offer. "You'd really do that?"

"Yes. I'd love to."

"Why are you trying so hard?"

"I just want to make things right between us. I want you to see how much I still love you."

"There's nothing between us worth saving," she says, that ice-cold tone back again. Her words slice into me, more painful than the knife. It's an effort to keep from wincing, from becoming angry, or from falling to my knees in front of her and begging her to tell me what the hell is running through that mind of hers.

"Of course there is," I say instead.

"It's too late, Seth."

"It's never too late." I reach for her arm again and lead her back into the bedroom. Picking her phone back up off the dresser, I use its light to shine our way back to bed.

Kendra makes herself comfortable beneath the covers and says, "There's a novel in the drawer of my nightstand."

I pull her novel out of her nightstand drawer and move next to her on the bed. Beside her, it's like nothing has happened. We're back to our normal selves—no murder, no time loop, no living hell.

I read her book aloud, flipping through the pages one by one, allowing myself to leave reality. Together, we travel through the pages into her historical romance where a rich, good-looking duke woos his beautiful ladylove.

After a while, Kendra leans her head against my shoulder. I'm using one hand to hold the book and the other to hold the phone light so I can see. I wish I could wrap an arm around her.

I half expect her to have the gun in hand when I'm not looking, ready to blow my brains out again, or another knife, or another way to kill me. But—nothing. She's patiently listening as if she doesn't have another care in the world.

Every now and then, I glance back up from the page to check on her, but she continues to look so relaxed, almost like she could fall asleep. Seeing her this way makes my tired body scream for sleep. All I want to do is close my eyes and pass out right alongside her.

A FEW CHAPTERS IN, my throat is becoming sore. I yawn. I know I can't fall asleep. I don't want to stop reading—I love this moment between us, but If I don't drink some water, I'm not going to be able to speak. And if I don't keep talking, I'll fall asleep.

I put the bookmark back in and close the book. "I'm just going to grab some water," I croak, lifting the light of the cell phone to shine around the bedroom. A bottle of water, two-thirds full, sits on the dresser.

Kendra hums to acknowledge me, making no effort to open her eyes, but sits up a little for me to get off the bed. I cross the room, chug the water until it's gone, then sigh in relief. My toes curl on top of the cold floor. I think about the house slippers I abandoned on my side of the bed, too hard to slip on when I'm running for my life.

Feeling better, I make my way back to the bed and cozy back up to Kendra.

She smiles up at me from her side of the bed. "Come here." She motions me closer.

"Why?" My eyebrows narrow at her. I'm no farther away than I was before... and now the look on her face is suggestive. I know better than to trust it. There's no way she's forgiven me this easily—all I've done is try to run her a bath and read her a book in bed. That's not possibly enough... is it?

"I want to kiss you," she says, tugging me closer.

And I know it's stupid. I *know* it is. But the part of me that misses my wife, misses kissing her, holding her, loving her— the idiot part of me gives in. I scoot across the bed so I'm nearly on top of her. I bend over her like a fool starved for her love and affection.

Kendra reaches an arm up around my neck, and for a heartbeat, her lips meet mine. Her intoxicating scent fills my senses, robbing my brain of all reason. The book is long forgotten.

She knows the moment I'm lost. Her arm tightens, pulling me closer, holding me in place. I reach around her waist, feeling for her other hand. Something cold and hard meets my fingertips. I try to back away, try to take in a breath to protest to ask—

Kendra positions the gun over my heart. "It *is* too late, Seth," she says before pulling the trigger.

CHAPTER
THIRTY-NINE

I want to cry like a child. I want to wail, to scream, to throw a tantrum until I get my way. *I'm at my wits' end here.* I'm running out of ideas and I'm *really* afraid that Kendra might be right. What if it *is* too late for us? What if nothing can be done to stop her or change her mind?

No. I can't think like that. I have to keep trying. If I have repeated lives, death doesn't touch me, it has to be for a reason. There has to be a *point*!

Before I can sulk until Kendra kills me and I have to restart *again*, I get up and get the knife and phone from her. She protests, denies trying to kill me, calls me crazy, *yada, yada, yada.*

I stand next to her side of the bed, looming over her with the knife, not *pointing* it at her, but I hold it in a way that lets her mind make some assumptions. "Where's the gun, Kendra?" I ask. "And please, for the love of God, spare me the denials." It's obviously here somewhere—in the room—within reach of the bed. That only leaves so many possibilities.

To my surprise, she doesn't bother denying it. Instead, she

says, "Okay. I'll tell you where it is if you tell me how you know about it. Did Nick tell you?"

Nick again! The same question as before, and now I *know* I was on to something. *Why did I give up the idea of Nick again?* I'm not even sure I remember. I scratch the back of my head, fighting to remember details that are now fuzzy.

"Yes. Nick told me. He also told me about your affair with Mark."

Kendra's lips press together. Her head tilts, then she smiles. "You know, Seth. I wouldn't be such a good liar if it wasn't for you teaching me."

I laugh at that, can't help myself. "You're *not* a good liar."

Her smile turns to a grin. "That must make two of us then."

I release a deep sigh, tired of her games. All I want is a straight answer—not a lie—*for once.* "Kendra, please."

"A deal's a deal," she says. "Tell me how you knew. And now I want to know how you know about Mark too... you don't seem as upset as I thought you would be."

I can't tell her the truth. She wouldn't understand—would either think I'd gone crazy or that I was lying again. I picture myself saying, "*Well, you see... when I walked in on you two in the gym shower, it kind of hit me in the face*"... or maybe saying, "*Don't worry, I killed him a couple of times already—will do it again if I get the chance.*"

Maybe I *am* a bad liar, but I don't have any other choice right now but to keep throwing stories at her until she buys one of them. "Megan," I say, and interestingly, it gets a reaction out of her.

"Megan told you?"

I shrug. "Yeah."

She tilts her head again, considering. "Megan knew about Mark... but she didn't know about any of this between us."

"Maybe I put two and two together on my own. Did you think about that?"

"Why don't you care more about the affair?" Kendra looks almost—*disappointed.*

I step closer to her. "I *do* care. All I want is for you to see how much I do. I don't want to lose you, Kendra. I want to put this behind us, to move forward with our lives, to not have to worry about you trying to kill me in my sleep for the rest of my days."

When I smile at her, she nods. "Okay."

"Okay... as in, we can move on?"

She smiles. "We can move on."

"Yes!" I throw my arms in the air, wanting to scream out the window. *It's over. It's finally over!* I don't feel any different— I guess we'll find out in the morning when I wake up and she's not trying to kill me.

Kendra chuckles when I throw the knife on top of the dresser and wrap her in a bear hug. "Tell me about Nick."

She backs away from me. "I thought we were moving on?"

"We are. Absolutely. But you're the one who keeps—" I clear my throat. "You're the one who brought him up."

Her smile falls. "Forget about Nick."

"Why did you ask about him then? If he's another lover—"

Kendra scoots across the mattress toward my side, trying to get farther away from me. I walk around the foot of the bed to meet her.

"Don't avoid me, Kendra. I know this is hard. Does Megan know about you and Nick? Is that what all this is about?"

She reaches for my lamp and tries to flip the switch, but it doesn't turn on. "Dammit," she hisses.

"The power's out." I turn the phone's flashlight on so we can see each other.

Kendra isn't trying to see me, though. She's opened my

nightstand drawer and is looking for something. "What are you—" I start and then I realize *what* she's looking for.

I'm too stunned at first to even move. *I can't believe she hid it on my side!* My vision blurs for a split second. Still holding the phone, I twist it down, shining the light anywhere else but where she needs it.

I'm too tired to see straight. I rub at my eyes, clear my vision, and finally see the button to turn the flashlight back off. Panting, I stand in the same spot, not knowing what else to say. *What is there to say?*

My wife still wants to kill me. She'll get the gun, she'll shoot me, and she'll keep doing it over and over. No amount of reasoning is going to work.

I hear the trigger pull back. I close my eyes, bracing myself. And she squeezes.

I open my eyes—*she missed!*

My ears are ringing. I can't hear a thing. But holy shit, Kendra missed me! In the black room, I can't see, I'm still blinded by the flashlight and then the flash of fire from the gun, but it doesn't matter. I have a small chance, a minuscule chance—

I reach for Kendra, for the gun, and she fires again.

At two in the morning, Kendra woke for her middle-of-the-night pee. She took one look at the phone on her nightstand to see the time, groaned, and rolled out of bed.

Her feet padded across the cold floor, toes curling when they hit the tile in the bathroom. She lifted the hem of her nightgown, ready to do her business when she noticed there was no toilet paper on the roll. *Dammit,* she thought, shivering against the cold night air.

She moved to look under the counter. And that's when something caught her eye. The box of pregnancy tests was under there. Kendra couldn't stop staring at the box. The urge to pee was overwhelming—she had to cross her legs to keep from having an accident.

When was my last—she couldn't remember. She knew she had to be wrong. Most likely. She grabbed one of the tests anyway.

Kendra opened the test and finally did her business.

A minute later, she saw two blue lines in the indicator window. Her breath caught. It couldn't be possible. *How—it had to be that one night*—she thought. Her heart galloped in her chest. She wanted to scream from the top of her lungs.

Kendra forgot all about the cold floor as she stood staring at the test in the bathroom. She finally decided she would go back to bed. She was probably dreaming—that was all. In the morning, she'd look at the test and it would only have one blue line instead of two.

MORNING CAME and there were still two blue lines. Seth woke up before her and saw the test sitting on top of the dresser as he was getting ready for work. He picked it up and stared at it. When he turned toward Kendra, she was sitting up in bed watching him.

"What's this?" he asked. "What does it mean?"

She gave a weak smile. "It means I'm pregnant."

He left the room without a word.

Kendra got up, got dressed, and eventually made it downstairs. Seth was fixing himself a cup of coffee. "Maybe we should—you know," he said, clearing his throat, waiting like she was supposed to read his mind.

"No... I don't know. What should we do?"

He stared at her, trying to think of the right words, unable to say them because he knew how angry she would be.

Her eyes nearly bulged from her skull as she waited for him to say something.

"The baby," he said.

"Yeah? What about the baby?" She would've slapped him across the face if he was within reach. The look on his face, his attitude, not a single positive thing to say—

He took a few steps toward her. "I'm sorry. I don't want to be insensitive, Kendra. I don't know how else to tell you how I'm feeling. I don't really—want kids."

"You don't want kids. Wow." She was dumbstruck, felt the blow right to her midsection—thought the baby might've heard it too. She felt her world spinning, her heart breaking. *Why would he be this way?* she thought. *This isn't Seth.*

"I'm sorry," he said lamely.

"You and I both know it's a lie. Why would you say that to me?"

Seth clenched his jaw. "It's not. I'm telling you how I feel here, Kendra."

"You listen to me, Seth McKnight. It's a little too fucking late for that. This baby is inside me whether you want it to be or not."

He went back to his coffee without arguing. "I'm sorry," he said again.

Tears fell from Kendra's eyes. She turned, unable to bear the sight of him. Then they parted ways, each heading to work without so much as a *goodbye.* For as long as she could, Kendra ignored the cramping and the blood that were slowly intensifying.

CHAPTER FORTY-ONE

efore I have a chance to think, I reach for the knife and phone. My exhaustion is only getting worse but somehow it finally dawns on me and I turn on the phone's flashlight, feeling like an idiot all those times it would've really come in handy. I ignore Kendra's glare as I come back to my nightstand. I get the drawer open, and there it is—the gun.

My hands are full with it, the knife, and the phone. I have them all but if Kendra rushed at me—let's just say I hope she doesn't try anything. She's still scowling at me from her side of the bed, but beneath the scowl, she almost seems dismayed.

That's right, queen. I've finally found it, and you're wondering how the hell I knew all your little secrets.

I leave her without a word. There's no more time for her games or her lies. She gave something away last time—something priceless. And it wasn't the gun. She gave me *Nick—and Megan.*

A FLASH of lightning lights up the barn in the rearview mirror. It looms in the night, silently watching me leave, and I wonder if the old building knows what I'm going through. If buildings could be aware of things, would they know about the time loop I'm trapped inside? Or would it be just like everyone else —clueless?

As I drive, I think about the obvious facts that have been staring me right in the face but I've been too tired *or dumb* to see: one, Megan and my wife are two peas in a pod—both liars, and two, Nick is not as innocent as he seems. The minute he handed me the scalpel for *just in case*, I should've known there was something off about him. I should've never held out hope that Kendra was wrong about them, that they could ever take my side, could *believe* me. I should've realized that my wife's best friend would have her back no matter what.

I could beat myself up all night about it, but it doesn't matter now. Kendra gave them up. She's as good as told me that they're in on it with her and now, I'm going to confront them. The pair of them won't fool me again.

ON THE FRONT STEP, I bang on the door over and over until a sleepy Nick finally answers with his baseball bat and flashlight in hand.

"What the hell is going on?" he asks, cracking the front

door open. He squints against the phone's light, shining his own through the crack, trying to see me better.

"Nick! Thank God, it's an emergency."

He sighs, irritated, like he's had to say this every night of his life. "I don't provide emergency services—"

"It's not for a pet." I take a step closer, adjusting the light so he can see my face a little better. "I'm Seth McKnight, Kendra's husband. We met—"

He opens the door the rest of the way. "Seth, how are you? It's been years." His eyes roam my face, and he finally seems to realize there's a real emergency. "Come in. What's wrong? Is it Kendra?"

He leads me through the entryway and living room, just like before. Now that I've been here a few times, I'm familiar with the layout of the house. He takes a seat on the couch, setting the flashlight on a side table so it shines toward the ceiling. The glow lights the room enough for us to see each other.

I remain standing. "Yeah, it's Kendra," I say, pulling out the gun with my free hand.

Nick pushes himself farther into the back of the couch, holding his hands up. "What do you want from me?"

"I know you know what's going on. Don't bother lying anymore. It's not going to work this time."

His bottom lip trembles when I cock the gun. "You have this all wrong. I swear on my life—on my *wife's* life, I don't know what you're talking about."

"Kendra has been planning to kill me."

"She *what?*"

"Spare me! God, I'm getting so tired of this shit!" I shoot the gun into the wall behind him.

Nick jumps in his seat, screaming for me to stop, for me to *not shoot.*

"As soon as you spill the beans, I'm out of here. You never have to see me again."

"I'll tell you anything you want to know," Nick sobs. "Please don't kill me."

"What do you know about her plan? Why does she want me dead so bad?"

"She—she—"

"She's sleeping with you?"

"No!"

"Then what?"

"She wants your life insurance?"

I don't have any life insurance, and he's making it sound like a question. I level the gun at his chest, tired of any more *lies*. "Lie to me one more time, and you're going to wish you hadn't," I warn.

Nick's pants turn dark as he loses control of his bladder. He looks mortified, terrified, and almost as miserable as I feel. "Please," he begs again. "I swear—"

I can't take any more of this. Just like Kendra, he's never going to tell me what I want to know. He's either too afraid to speak or he doesn't know anything anyway. I shoot Nick twice in the chest, then aim for his head and pull the trigger.

A high-pitched scream comes from behind me. I turn to see Megan, one arm wrapped around herself, the other trembling, holding a candle. Tears streaming down her stricken face.

I level the gun at her. "You know what I want to know."

She throws the candle at me from across the room. Hot wax pours onto the floor as the candle sails through the air toward me. I dodge it easily, listening to the glass shatter behind me. The flame, still burning, sets the carpet on fire.

"I don't know anything," Megan says, backing away.

"She said you did. She said *both* of you did."

"She was lying."

"That may be. But I think you're lying now."

Megan looks at the flames behind me, quickly spreading.

"We can put it out," I say. "Just tell me what I need to know."

Her lips thin. She wipes away stray tears. "You just killed my husband. Do you really think I'm going to help you?"

"I think you will to save your home. To save your own life —" I eye her up and down as she tries to shield herself.

Megan pauses and thinks. Smoke is starting to fill the air between us. If she waits too much longer, neither of us will have air to breathe, and her house might be beyond saving.

"Okay," she finally says. "What you need to know—is that I called Kendra the minute Nick let you in. She'll be here any minute, and you can take up whatever the hell this is with her."

My teeth grind together. "Tell me why she wants me dead."

Megan laughs. "Maybe because you're an asshole?"

"Tell me the plan!"

She takes another step back. "No."

I shoot the gun at Megan. The bullet hits its mark, straight through her forehead. I watch her drop dead on the floor as the flames on the carpet begin to climb up the furniture and walls. There's nothing else for me here.

Leaving Nick and Megan in the burning room, I make my way back to the front door. I open it, hating myself for the way things went. Now that they're dead, I either have to find another place to start—the school again probably—or I have to wait until I reset again—not looking forward to that.

Kendra is on the stoop, one hand reaching toward the door handle. Her eyes meet mine and before I have a chance to blink, she plunges a knife through my heart. "I was hoping I'd run into you," she says.

I stumble forward and drop, gasping for breath.

Kendra pulls me back inside, and I'm too weak to stop her or to even try. Just as I think she's going to stab me again, she leaves me alone to bleed out in the entryway of the burning house or burn to death—whichever comes first.

Luckily for me, I didn't have to endure being burned alive. But that Kendra would want me to—it's somehow colder than just stabbing me or shooting me. The amount of pain that I would suffer If I hadn't bled out—

She wants you dead, remember?

Being burned alive is more than that though. It's a whole new level of evil.

I get the knife, the phone, the gun. I make it downstairs, get the keys, and get into my truck. Lightning strikes in the exact same way as last time, lighting up the barn in my rearview mirror. The old building watches my tires spit rocks as I head back into town.

A LONG NIGHT passes while I battle against sleep trying to draw me into its fold. *I've done it before—more than once—I can do it again.* And I do. I survive the night, awake, and watch the sunrise from the school parking lot.

I know that Nick and Megan are alive again—just like me, they've been reset. Knowing when I kill them, I'm *not really* killing them—in addition to the loop, makes me almost numb to death. Instead of dealing with them again, trying to get more information, I think I'll take my search elsewhere. The way I see it, there are only two other people for me to speak with—Nicolas and Mark.

Nicolas seemed like a nice enough kid, straightforward and willing to help. He didn't seem to be holding anything back as far as I could tell. Mark was helpful in his own way too, although he was closer to Kendra than I like to think about.

He would know more than Nicolas, I believe, and if nothing else, I can have the pleasure of killing him again. *Why not?* When everything will just reset all over again the minute Kendra gets me within her sights. He'll be alive and well and screwing her all over again, no matter how many times I kill him.

When the time's right, I make my way into the boy's locker room. I wait behind the same row of lockers as before for the motion lights to turn back off. Eventually, the shower turns off and Kendra leaves. When I have Mark all alone, I make my move.

I approach from behind as he's pulling clothes out from his locker, pistol whipping the back of his head. He falls forward into the open locker, crying out from the surprise and pain. His naked body is pushed halfway inside. He seems to be trying to crawl farther in it to get away from me. The sight of a grown man, as big as myself, trying to crawl into a half-size locker is almost comical.

Blood is on the barrel of the gun. I got him good—enough to scare the shit out of him, but not good enough. Reaching back, I swing at him again, giving him another good blow, this time to his back.

Mark drops to the floor, trying to cover himself with his arms. "Stop! Stop!" he yells. "What do you want?"

"Are you ready to answer some questions?"

"Yes! Just stop!"

I stand back enough for him to sit up. He looks up at me from the floor, and from the look in his eyes, I can tell he's not sure yet if he can trust that I won't hit him again. *Guess he's not a total idiot.*

"Tell me about Kendra's plan," I say.

"Which one would that be?"

"Any one you're familiar with. And don't be a smart-ass."

Mark lowers his head to look at the floor. "I take it you're her old man."

"Younger than you, from the looks of it, asshole."

He looks back up at me, a little more fire behind his eyes. "Don't take it out on me, alright, man. She's *your* wife, she wasn't satisfied, apparently. She came onto *me* and—I mean, look at her! Like I'm going to turn her away? Yeah, right."

I have a sudden urge to blow his head off his shoulders. My jaw is clamped down so tight I can feel the crown in the back of my mouth protest. My finger tightens on the trigger as I stare down at him, into those eyes that have not an ounce of remorse.

"You're playing with fire, friend. Tell me what she has planned."

"I'm not your friend. And I don't know what the hell you're talking about."

"Why does she want me dead?"

"Is it because you're a dick?"

This guy's attitude is wearing my patience thin. I liked him better when he was trying to crawl inside the locker like a rodent scurrying away. He's got cajones, that's for sure, at least now that he's facing me man to man.

The sound of kids comes from far away—inside the gym. Mark and I wait for them to stop screwing around and leave. He has a chance to call out, but he doesn't take it. The moment passes, and it's quiet again. *This is taking too long! I've been here too long!*

"Were you going to run away together?" I ask.

"No. I—have a wife too. I don't want her to know about this, either. How you're acting—she'd be even worse."

Then you'd deserve it, buddy. Who's the real dick here? "So, you don't know why she wants me dead?"

"No idea."

"What *do* you know then?" *I'm standing here, wasting my time again!*

"Look," he says. "All I know is that she comes in here when she wants to fuck. We don't talk, don't *plan* anything except the next time we're going to meet. It's a thrill—that's all. The only ones who know about us are Nicolas, he's the other gym teacher, and Megan, another teacher here at the school—she's Kendra's friend. I'm sure a couple of the kids have suspected something, but—" He shrugs as if that's supposed to explain everything.

"Okay," I say, nodding. "Thank you, Mark. For your honesty."

He sighs, relieved. "Can I get up now? I need to get ready for class."

"I think you might be a little late today." I raise the gun and *finally* pull the trigger. Mark's head explodes into the locker, and I head back to my truck, on the verge of collapse.

CHAPTER
FORTY-THREE

I've seen it all before, heard it all before—the same people, the same lines, the same *lies, excuses, stories,* over and over and over. *Wasting time, wasting time!* I've talked to them all, reasoned with them, begged for help, for understanding, for—*anything!*

No one knows a goddamned thing.

Now what?

The first thing I have to do is get the hell away from the school. Shifting into gear, I drive across town, brainstorming ideas. I'm going around in circles, doing everything over and over, getting the same answers from everyone's mouths—everything is starting to blur together.

I pull the truck over on the side of the road, my head throbbing. I lean against the steering wheel, closing my eyes. *Just for a minute.*

Kendra mentioned Megan and Nick.

Mark mentioned Megan and Nicolas.

My eyes open. *Megan is the common denominator.* She has to know something—has to! But how do I get her to talk? I've tried asking, that didn't work. I've tried using force, that didn't work either.

I need to get her alone. If she's away from Nick—not just in another room, but if he's nowhere *near* us, I might be able to get more out of her. I just hope this time I can tell when she's full of shit. And if she *really* doesn't know anything... I don't know what I'm going to do.

THE DAY PASSES. I'm parked along the curb in front of Nick and Megan's house. Waiting. I thought staying up all night was boring, but this—this is a whole new level of mind numbness. I don't have a choice though. I can't confront her at school.

I'm expecting to stick around until at least four or five o'clock before she shows up, but around noon, Megan's car pulls into the driveway. I slink down lower in my seat as she looks around outside. Her eyes drift toward the truck, she pauses, then before she can make it inside the house, I get out.

"Megan, wait."

"Seth?"

"Yeah. It's me. I'm sorry to show up like this, I really need to talk."

"How long have you been waiting for me?"

"Not very long." I rub the back of my neck, trying to ease some of the tension sitting in the truck for half the day has caused.

"Come in," Megan says, leading me through the front door.

The power is back on now. She flips the light switches and offers me a drink. I settle myself up at the kitchen table, the idea of sitting on the couch again—the memory of a dead Nick still fresh in my mind—a little too uncomfortable.

"How did you know I'd be home early today?" Megan asks.

"I didn't. I wasn't sure when—"

"Did you hear about the murder?"

"No..."

"One of the teachers was murdered today. Police were doing interviews for hours. The school was evacuated." Her eyes watch me, unblinking. She's pretty sure she knows what's going on, but she's trying to read me to make sure.

"I'm sorry to hear that. Listen, I need your help, Megan. Kendra is trying to kill me, and I don't want to wind up like that teacher at your school."

Her eyes narrow and finally blink. "That doesn't sound like Kendra. Have you called the police?"

"I'm going to. I just—" *God, not the same conversation all over again!* "I need to know who Nick is. Kendra mentioned him, and I think you're the only one besides her who can help."

"The only Nick I know is *my* Nick."

"Is there anyone at the school or anywhere else? Anyone at all that you can think of?"

"Nicolas is the other gym teacher...."

"Besides him?"

She throws up her arms. "I don't know. I'm sorry, Seth. Why does this matter anyway? What's this have to do with her trying to kill you?"

"You know... the funny thing here—is that you're not even surprised." I pull the gun out from the back of my pants to level it at her. "Tell me what you know, Megan. No more bullshitting, or I'll blow your fucking brains all over the wall."

Her jaw sags open. Her eyes move from the barrel of the gun to me and back again as she wraps her arms around herself. "I don't know any other Nicks," she says.

I cock the gun.

"But—" she goes on. "Kendra mentioned talking to a Nicole."

"And what exactly did she say about Nicole?"

"Nothing, really. She just came up in conversation once when Kendra canceled on me. She said she had to look after Nicole, and I thought it was just one of her students."

"She didn't say anything else about her?"

"No. Not that I can remember."

"How long ago was that?"

"I'm not sure... maybe a week or so."

"Okay... and she just mentioned Nicole the once?"

"Yes, Seth. Do you think that could be who you're looking for?"

"Maybe," I say, then I pull the trigger.

I leave, knowing exactly who Nicole is and where to find her. I feel like an idiot for not thinking of her before—she should've at least crossed my mind! How did I not think—

It doesn't matter. I can't even be mad at myself anymore, because I've finally found *Nick* and *she* is right at home, where I left her.

Weekends are the worst, Kendra thought, rolling over in bed. Most people looked forward to them, but Kendra was at a point in her life where she wished the week would never end. She waited for Monday the way most waited for Friday because work was a happier place than home and had been for some time.

Her phone vibrated on top of her nightstand as a message came through.

What are you doing today?

Kendra looked at the empty bed beside her before texting Megan back.

Not sure yet. Might catch up on some reading.

Megan's response was almost instant.

Ugh. Lucky! I'm at a stupid brunch thing.

Not in the mood to talk, she set the phone on her mattress

and stared at the spot that Seth should be. She didn't want to think about why he never stayed in bed longer than he had to or how he never wanted to be alone in the house at all with her unless it was to eat or sleep. They were going through a rough patch—that was all. After seven years of marriage, wouldn't it be weird if they weren't?

Everyone goes through this, she told herself, trying to make the bitter feeling in the pit of her stomach subside. She didn't know how long it had been there now, festering like an old sore that wouldn't heal. No matter what she told herself, it never seemed to want to go away.

Her phone buzzed again—another message from Megan.

Make Seth take you out.

Kendra thought about it. It was a good idea... besides the fact that they hadn't gone out since she couldn't remember when. And besides the fact that he seemed to never want to be in the same room as her these days. She responded:

Maybe. Eat some food for me.

She went back to sleep. By the time she got up, got dressed, and went downstairs, it was nearly lunchtime. Seth was nowhere to be seen—nowhere in the house. Kendra moved to the front window to look out at the yard.

The barn doors were closed, but his truck was in the driveway. She thought about going out there to him to extend an olive branch of sorts. *Maybe he'll want to go out for lunch if I ask,* she thought. He'd been up all morning—way earlier than even the first time she woke up; she thought he had to be hungry.

AS SHE WALKED across the driveway to the barn, she thought about what she was in the mood for. A burger didn't sound good to her... pasta? No. She thought about a plate of tacos with some homemade guac, and her mouth started to water. *Guess I know where we're going*, she thought with a smile.

Kendra reached for the handle of the barn door. She pulled—the door wouldn't open. She frowned, looked around the yard, then looked back. "Seth?" she called. She tried to pull harder, but the door still wouldn't budge.

"Seth!" Kendra called. She put her ear against the door, listening for movement inside. She hammered her fist against the door a few times. "Seth! Open the door!" She waited, thinking maybe he was just in the back or under the car or something, but no response came. Kendra turned to leave when the door opened.

Seth stood in the doorway, looking confused. "What's wrong?"

"Why was the door locked? What are you doing?"

"I'm working on my car."

"Why was the door locked?" Kendra repeated, eyebrows raised at the guilty look on his face. She noticed how he seemed to be blocking her from going inside.

"It must've jammed," he said, flushing.

"Let me come inside." She started to move forward, but Seth stayed blocking her entry.

"Why do you want in here? You always have to do that, you know. I can't just do something without you sticking your nose in it."

"I just want to see what you're working on."

"Why?" His defensive tone had grown into something accusing and cold. It sent chills up Kendra's spine the way he was looking at her.

"I'm just curious," she said.

"Is that why you're out here bugging me? Because you're *curious?* Sorry you're bored, Kendra. Get your own fucking hobby and leave mine alone." He stepped back into the barn.

The door didn't close behind him, but Kendra still hesitated. Her face burned. She didn't know whether to follow him in there and make him think twice about talking to her that way—or if maybe he was right. She was *interested*, not nosy—but she didn't know what to think.

All she'd wanted was to invite him to lunch, to do something *together*. One thing was for sure—lunch was out of the question now. He was surly and defensive—clearly didn't want her hanging around. *Fine*, she thought, leaving back for the house. She picked a book and got in the car, ready to have lunch by herself.

Even though she hated eating alone at restaurants, it was better than being stuck here with him. Whatever Seth was up to out there—she would leave him alone. Maybe it was for the best anyway.

When I get home, Kendra isn't back yet. If what Megan said was true, then she's off work and she can show back up here at any time. But that's okay. I don't mind if she comes home early this time. I've got bigger fish to fry, and Kendra isn't going to get in my way.

Instead of going into the house, I head through the rain, across the driveway, toward the barn. By the door, there's a light switch. I flip it to shine the barn lights.

The barn is large enough to house several horses or other livestock, but neither Kendra nor myself were ever interested in adopting animals and taking care of them. Instead, the barn is full of garden supplies, holiday storage, old pictures, and rusty car parts.

Once upon a time, I had plans to build a project car, and up until this afternoon, *I thought* Kendra believed I was *still* working on one. I spend a lot of my spare time in the barn, tinkering with an old beat-up engine, an empty body, wiring, a radio—anything to make me *look* busy. Because really, I couldn't give a damn about the car. Its only purpose now is to give me an excuse to come out here.

I walk through the barn, past the workbench, past the

engine stand, past the lift, until I reach one of the horse stalls filled with storage. There are a few boxes stacked precisely—they look filled to the brim, heavy too. I take hold of the nearly *empty* boxes and move them aside, revealing a small square door in the floor of the barn.

One more glance around just to make sure, and I head down the narrow steps. On the way down, I tug on the pull cord hanging above the stairs to light the steps beneath my feet. There's a room below—about the size of a small bedroom, already dimly lit by a bedside lamp. There, on the bed, is Nicole.

She sits up when I enter, expecting food.

"Shit, I'm sorry," I say.

"I haven't eaten all day."

"I know. I have a lot going on, and I forgot. I'll run up to the house and get you something."

"Thank you, Seth."

"But first—I need to ask you something." I come the rest of the way down the stairs into the room, and sit across from her in a wingback chair.

Nicole tilts her head up to me. "What is it?"

"Has anyone been to see you down here?"

Her face instantly flushes from the top of her forehead down to her neck. She doesn't have to speak a word. I already know the answer.

"Only you," Nicole says.

"I see." I let silence pass between us.

Nicole plays with her hands in her lap for a minute, then says, "Okay, Kendra came down here. She asked me not to say anything. I'm sorry."

And just like that—everything I've done, all this effort put in to find the answer—I've finally found it. *This* is why she wanted me dead. "What did you two talk about?" I ask, my mind reeling with possibilities.

"She asked me questions, like if I was comfortable or cold or hungry, things like that."

"And what did you tell her?"

"I told her I was fine, of course. I'm warm and fed every day. I don't need anything else."

"And is that true, Nicole? Are you happy?"

She pauses for a moment, still flushed. "I do get lonely..." she says.

"How often has Kendra been coming down?"

"Every day."

"Every day... for how long?"

"I'm not sure. A while."

And that explains everything. "Does she call you Nick?"

Nicole smiles. "Yes. I think it's funny."

"Listen, Nicole. Things have changed. Kendra isn't going to be able to visit you anymore. I'm sorry."

Her smile falls. "Did I do something wrong?"

"No, not at all. It isn't your fault."

"I tried to be quiet. I didn't make any noises, just like you told me. I was just reading a book when she came down."

I place a hand on her shoulder to reassure her. "I know this isn't your doing. Kendra is stubborn. I'm sure she followed me, and that's how she found you."

Nicole looks at me with tears pooling in her eyes. "Why can't she come back?"

"Because she's doing very bad things up there, and I'm worried she might try to hurt you if she keeps coming back."

She shakes her head. "No, I don't think she would—"

"Don't argue, Nicole. I'm sorry you feel lonely. I'll think about getting you a friend. Would you like that?"

"Yes. Very much."

"Maybe... a kitten?"

Her eyes brighten. "A white one!"

I laugh at her excitement. "Maybe. No promises."

Nicole gives me a hug, already knowing I'll give her anything her heart desires. Well, *almost* anything.

"Nicole, there's one more thing." I hold her at arm's length so she knows this is serious. "Kendra—did you know Kendra planned on hurting me?"

Her eyes are saucers. Her mouth falls open, ready to lie, but she stops. Crying now, she nods. "Yes. She told me."

"What did she tell you?"

"She said she had to stop you—that it was the only way for her to save me, or else you would kill both of us." Nicole's eyes shift to look behind me.

I turn to see Kendra standing on the open staircase, drained of all color.

"Come in, wife. Perfect timing."

Kendra comes down the stairs to join us. When she sits at the foot of Nicole's bed, Nicole grabs hold of her hand and beams up at her, her tears already drying on her cheeks. Kendra gives her a weak smile. "Hey Nick, how are you feeling today?"

"A little scared."

Ignoring Kendra's grim expression, I say, "I was just telling *Nicole* that you won't be able to visit her anymore. You weren't supposed to be here at all."

"He said you've been doing bad things," Nicole says.

"*I've* been doing bad things? That's a little hypocritical, isn't it, Seth?" Kendra glares at me.

"Nicole is a good girl, Kendra. She told me all about your plan—all about *why*."

"Don't you think we should have this talk in private?" Kendra hisses.

"I don't think so. I don't feel like getting murdered today, and Nicole is already well aware of your intentions. You need to let me explain."

Kendra stands. "I'm not going to sit here and have this conversation in front of her."

Nicole's eyes pass between us, filling with tears again.

Kendra's right—we shouldn't be arguing like this in front of her, but dammit, it's the only way I can be sure she won't kill me. It's also the only way I can get her to talk. I don't know what I'm doing. Now that I know who *Nick* is, what the plan is, what's next?

I'm starting to have a sinking feeling that someone needs to die—and *that* someone isn't me.

I'm not a religious man, but the story of Abraham comes to mind. It's one of the more popular Bible stories—a man forced to sacrifice his son, and at the last minute, God says, "Just kidding," or something along those lines, and he winds up not having to do it after all. I'm not sure how I heard the story or why I'm thinking of it now—but I wonder... what if that's what I'm meant to do with Nicole—if the loop is really about *her* and not Kendra? If I'm supposed to go so far as to make my sacrifice, and in the end, she won't really be dead?

I decide to let Kendra leave. She'll only try to stop me.

She takes a few steps toward the stairs and turns back. "You know what? Nick, come with me." She reaches her hand out toward Nicole.

Nicole's eyes widen. She looks back to me.

"She's not going anywhere, Kendra."

"Why not? Why don't you explain to us both why she's trapped in this hole in the ground? And what's going to happen to her, Seth? She's going to stay down here forever?"

"I don't want to go," Nicole says, turning bright red, watching me. She scoots down beneath her covers, flattening herself against the mattress.

"See? She doesn't want to go anywhere."

"Nick, this is your chance. Let's get out of here while we can together. Seth isn't going to stop us. We can do it *together*. I'll make sure he doesn't come after us now. Let's be free."

Nicole clamps her eyelids shut so she doesn't have to see Kendra's hand beckoning for her.

"Stop harassing her and go."

"She's brainwashed! I'm not harassing her; I'm trying to save her!"

"Leave, Kendra."

Kendra clenches her fists, considers, then rushes toward Nicole. She rips her from beneath the covers, Nicole fighting her the whole time.

"Stop!" she cries, trying to bat Kendra off.

Watching the struggle is hard. Seeing Both of them this way is hard. Pulling the gun out and making myself ready is even harder.

I have to do it. It's the only way.

"Don't you see?" Kendra pleads. "He's going to kill you!"

"He wouldn't do that! He loves me! He takes care of me."

"You're all alone down here, Nick."

"He's going to bring me a kitten! A white one."

Kendra finally lets go of her. She shakes her head, crying freely. "Silly girl. How naive you are." She points toward me, and I pull the trigger before Nicole can turn around to see me.

Nicole collapses, blood pooling around her, soaking into the concrete floor.

Kendra only stares at me, still crying.

I wait for something to happen—to feel different, to be reset again, to wake up in bed next to Kendra—*no more loop*—

But nothing happens. Blood continues to flow from Nicole. Kendra and I continue to stand in stilted silence as the child in Nicole's body dies along with his mother.

What have I done?

"You were going to buy her a cat," Kendra whispers.

"I told her maybe."

"You bastard."

"Kendra, you don't understand."

"She didn't deserve this—" She holds her arms out, gesturing to the entire situation. "She was just a girl!"

"I found her! I saved them! It's not what I wanted. I wanted to—"

"You never cared about anyone but yourself!" she screams.

"No! You're wrong—"

Kendra hurries for the stairs. She's halfway up before I realize what she's planning, and by the time I rush after her, I'm only able to grab hold of her foot. She shakes it, but I hang on, pulling her back down.

With a scream, Kendra uses her other foot to kick me in the face. I fall backward, landing next to Nicole's body with a bloodied nose and mouth. Kendra makes it through the door and slams it shut. I hear the sound of her moving storage boxes on top, sealing me in.

With effort, I get myself back up the stairs. I push against the now latched door but whatever she's put on top of it is too heavy. "Kendra! Don't leave me here!" I use my shoulder and my back, applying as much pressure as I can, using all the strength I have left—but it's no use.

She's gone. And I'm trapped down here alone with Nicole and her child within.

I wish she would let me explain. Would the gun do me any good? I could shoot at the door, but I don't think it would matter. Whatever is up there would *still* be up there.

I could—*reset* myself. But—if I'm right about the loop being done and over with, well then, I guess that means *I'll* be done and over with too. But what if I'm wrong? Nothing happened, nothing changed. I didn't feel any different when Nicole died. *Still tired...*

What if the loop isn't over? I could just reset myself, get out of this situation, and Nicole and the baby could be alive again, no one the wiser. *There might be another way—*

No. There is no other way. I place a hand against my temple that aches more than my broken nose. This lack of sleep is killing me more than Kendra ever could with any kind of weapon. It's getting harder for me to stop and think rationally—to concentrate.

I pace the small room, avoiding Nicole and her blood, trying to think of something, anything, to get me out of this. There's no other way out, no way to call for help—no one to call. I'm not worried about the police. Kendra is going to leave me down here to die. She's going to let me starve to death or die from dehydration.

Or let me kill myself.

"Well, Nicole. Let's see if you were the key to ending this nightmare."

Pulling the gun out again, I decide to take the faster way out.

CHAPTER FORTY-EIGHT

I'm conscious again. And I know I've failed. I'm somewhat relieved—I'm not dead, after all, but I'm also back to square one *again*.

Nicole wasn't the key. Suicide wasn't the key either. So what now? I'll tell you what now. Now, I'm going to kill *everyone* and see if that works. Maybe if everyone's dead, fate will finally cut me some slack.

Knife, phone, gun, keys, truck. I don't need the phone or the knife now—the gun and the bullets will do what I need, but I still bring them with. Better to have them and not need them. Plus, it's the only way to get out of the house since Kendra is not on the list of *everyone*.

My first stop is to see Nick and Megan. Just like previously, I pound on the door until he answers with his bat and flashlight in hand. I shoot him point blank as soon as he has the door cracked.

He collapses in the entryway, and I step over his fallen body, headed for the stairs. Things are so much easier now that I don't need information. All I need is to get this over and done with so I can move on with my life.

On the second floor, Megan is cowering in the bedroom with her cell phone next to her ear. "I'm calling the police!" she cries.

"Tell them hi for me." I put a bullet in her head. When the phone falls to the floor, I see that it's not the police she's called—but Kendra.

I pick up the phone with Kendra screaming through the speaker. "Sorry, Kendra. Megan isn't available right now."

"You bastard! Leave her alone!"

"She's gone, Kendra. Nick too."

"Why! Why are you doing this? *I'm* the one you should be after. Not them! Not anyone else!"

"They were in on it the whole time. What kind of people know you're fucking around and don't tell the husband? What kind of people do that, Kendra? And nobody is fooling me, okay? I know they knew about you trying to kill me too. This is over. Tonight."

I end the call before she has a chance to respond. I don't want to hear her spout any more lies or excuses or anything else. It's over, like I said. So, I move out of the house, back to my truck, and head to Nicolas's house.

I hate to do it. I kind of liked him, really. His mom was whatever, but I didn't have a problem with either of them. I'm sorry they're a part of this, but it's the way the dice rolled.

I pound on the door until the woman answers. Just like Nick, I shoot her point blank. She's bigger than he was, though, and when she falls, she blocks the door from opening. It takes me a minute to shove it open and get past her.

Down the hall, in his bedroom, Nicolas is still sleeping. I

almost laugh seeing him snoring open mouthed on his twin-size bed. He looks just like a kid—*is* a kid pretty much.

"Sorry, guy," I whisper before I put two bullets in him.

Mark is next on my list, and he's one that I'm really looking forward to. Since I don't know where he lives, I have to wait until morning and meet him at the school.

I'M OUT OF BULLETS, but it's not a problem. I still have Kendra's handy-dandy knife. The clock strikes six thirty, and I make my move.

I'm going in early this time. No sense waiting and making myself listen to Kendra and him in the shower all over again. There's no reason he needs to be alive long enough to enjoy that.

In the locker room, the motion lights flash on as I walk through. Something seems—different. I keep going to my usual spot at the back of a row of particular lockers—and then it hits me. The shower isn't on.

You're early, remember?

Right. I'm early.

I release a breath, deciding that I don't need to take up my spot behind the lockers after all. Instead, I head toward Mark's office. I get there, knock on the door, wait.

No answer.

I peek through the slats of the mini blinds. It doesn't look like there's even a light on. *Fuck!* Mark isn't here. And he's not going to be here today. Because Kendra warned him that I was coming.

Stupid, stupid, stupid! I should've never talked to her on Megan's phone. I gave myself away like an idiot.

Now what?

Well, one thing's for sure. Mark is going to die. I didn't just murder four people for nothing. He's next, no matter what Kendra tries to pull.

I decide to break into the office. I was able to find Nicolas's home information here before, and it works like a charm again. Lying on the desk is a phone bill for Mark—address front and center. *Maybe next time, stick to e-statements, Mark, buddy.*

I have the bill in hand, ready to leave and get going when something stops me. I look down at the top sheet of paper that begins listing all the phone numbers Mark has been in contact with for the month of September. My wife's phone number is on there...

I start flipping through the pages. Hers is one of only a handful of others. He said he was married...

He is cheating on his wife—maybe not a happy marriage.

Maybe. But something tells me there's more going on here than just *having fun*. He's playing this off as unimportant, but why would Kendra warn a booty call?

My fist tightens around the phone bill. Ready to find out more about what's *really* going on between this man and my wife, I leave the locker room and get back into my truck.

CHAPTER FORTY-NINE

As I come up the walk to Mark's house, I see that one of his front windows is open. Raised voices come from inside. I could continue to the front door, mind my own business, and kill him like I intended, but I think I'd rather do a little closer snooping first.

I get close to the window, tucking myself in as close to the house as I can get to avoid the rain as much as possible. The drapes are drawn back a ways to let some air in, and through the window screen, I see Mark and a woman—his wife, I presume. They're in a bedroom from the looks of it. "You don't have to do this," she says to him, trying to grab on to his shoulders.

Mark pushes her off and crosses the room to where a suitcase lies open on the bed. "So you'd rather I stay and get killed?" he says, taking a handful of socks from the dresser and throwing them into the suitcase.

"We can talk to the man—explain."

"There is no explaining to a spurned husband, Sadie."

Her face goes beet red. "No, only a spurned wife, I suppose."

"Listen, I'm sorry. I didn't want it to be like this. I don't—

I'm willing to talk about things, but right now, this man is on my ass like white on rice. If he figures out where I live, we're *all* in danger."

"It's just like you to get involved with a woman who has a crazy husband!" she screams.

Mark moves to the closet, where he grabs a few shirts off hangers. He keeps packing without responding.

"I'm sorry," his wife says, slightly calmer. "Please, Mark. I forgive you. Don't leave us like this. What am I supposed to tell Christina? If we can make it work, maybe this woman and her husband can too." She reaches for his shoulders again.

Mark spins on her. "You don't understand, Sadie. If I'm here, we all *die*. If I'm gone, none of us do."

Tears and snot roll down the woman's face. She stands in the middle of the room, sobbing her heart out, wanting to lean into Mark, but he continues holding her at a distance. They stare at each other for a few moments before he lets her go and moves back to packing.

My heart goes out to her. She looks completely destroyed, and he doesn't seem to give a damn. I didn't know it was possible, but it makes me hate him a little more. *I'm sorry your husband's a piece of shit, lady.*

She starts to plead with him again, but I've heard enough. I take a quick glance around to make sure no one is walking down the sidewalk and no neighbors are sitting on their front porch—there's not—then I pop the screen off the open window.

I slide the window open farther, enough to fit through, and I wait, listening for their continued conversation. It's hard to believe—*the window is right there*—but they don't notice a thing. Mark is too worried about packing and getting the hell out of there, while his wife is too worried about convincing him to stay.

When I'm sure that neither are aware of my presence, I grab on to the windowsill and pull myself up into the bedroom. Before I'm all the way in, Mark's wife lets out a high-pitched scream. I swing my leg over and in just as Mark rushes to shut the window on me.

Before my fingers are smashed, I pull the gun from my back pocket and aim it right at his face. "Don't," I say.

He pauses and weighs the possibility of me shooting him—hitting him—before he can lock me out. Finally realizing that even if he does get the window shut, I won't be stopped for long—a bullet can go right through glass—Mark takes a step back with his hands up.

Once all the way in, I close the window behind me.

A little girl enters the room. "Mommy, I heard you scream."

"Christina, go back to your bedroom," Mark says.

"But Mommy—"

"I said now, Christina."

"Mommy's fine, baby," the woman says. "I thought I saw a rat, that's all."

"Eww!"

"Christina!" Mark barks.

The little girl breaks down into tears, running from the room.

"You didn't have to yell at her," I say.

"Mind your own fucking business. Let me worry about my kid."

"What do you want?" the woman asks.

I pause with the gun still pointed toward Mark. *What do I want?* It's a good question—one I thought I knew the answer to. Five minutes ago, I *did* know the answer, and I suppose it hasn't changed—*much.*

"I assume you know why I'm here?" I direct my question toward the woman but Mark answers.

"Kendra told me."

His wife flinches at Kendra's name. Her eyes meet mine, and I'm not quite sure what I see in them—deep down, beneath the grief. Embarrassment? A want of revenge? Maybe she secretly, deep, deep down, *wants* me to kill him.

"I had some questions for you, but I think I've heard all I need to hear."

"What kinds of questions?" Mark asks, his voice quaking.

I shrug. "Questions like—are you running away with Kendra? And why would she bother to warn you about me if you were just fuck buddies?"

His wife's face drains of all color. Her jaw drops.

Mark's lips pinch together. He looks at his wife. "It's not like that—"

"Whatever it's like," I say, "I don't really want to know anymore." I level the gun at his chest and pull the trigger.

Nothing happens.

Dammit! I forgot—no more bullets.

I grin at Mark, who's pissed himself. "Just kidding." I throw the gun at his head, then rush at him.

His wife screams again but stands back while I hit his head with my fist over and over. Mark puts up a fight, swinging his own fists at me, trying to pry me off, but I had the upper hand from the get-go. We scuffle around the floor, bumping into the furniture, taking turns getting hit, until finally I get him into a choke hold.

"Let him go! Let him go!" the woman screams.

I hang on until Mark passes out. I leave the bedroom to find the kitchen, ignoring the woman's cries. I grab a knife and go back to the room to finish the job.

She tries to block me. *The woman has balls.* But she's taking for granted that I'm here for him. She doesn't understand that I'll do anything necessary. Rather than fight her off, I stab her first. Then I finish Mark.

I still feel the same. Nothing noticeable has changed and I have no idea if the loop is broken.

Before I leave, I go into the little girls' room. She's on her floor playing with dolls, still crying from being yelled at. She turns to me. "Who are you?"

"My name's Seth." A pause. "Can I be your friend?"

She sniffs and wipes at her cheeks. "Okay."

"You want to come to my house to play?"

"Okay," she says again.

I reach for her hand, and she takes it.

In the middle of a Saturday night, Kendra woke up to the sound of what she thought was a faint screaming. She sat up in bed. Seth's space next to her was vacant. She started to call for him—then she remembered he was doing overtime tonight.

Kendra wiped the sleep from her eyes, trying to focus. As she did, the scream came again, slightly louder. It sounded like—"Help!" but was too faint for her to be completely sure.

She got up on her knees to look out the window behind her, shielding her eyes against the glass, trying to get a good view, but it was too dark outside. It looked like—

With a gasp, she jumped back from the window. *Someone is in the driveway,* she thought. She didn't know who—man or woman, she couldn't tell, but there was no mistaking the shape of the figure moving in the dark. It was a person.

Kendra moved to the closet where the bedroom safe was. She punched in the code and shuffled through old paperwork until she found what she was looking for. Seth's 9mm handgun sat next to a clip of bullets. She grabbed them and headed downstairs.

KENDRA SHONE her flashlight through the front window, lighting up the outside area closest to the house. She twisted it back and forth across the yard, but the figure she saw earlier was either gone or farther in the shadows. She didn't hear any more—there it was again—a cry for help, loud and clear this time.

When she stepped outside, she noticed one of the barn doors wide open. Inside the barn was just as dark as the night outside but—*Why is the door open?* she wondered.

She began to head that way when the figure stepped out from around the house. Kendra startled when she heard the footsteps so close. She shone the flashlight right in the person's face. "Who are you?" She held the gun out. "I have a gun!"

The figure spoke. "Please help me."

Kendra lowered the flashlight to see a young woman—possibly a teenager. She was dirty, hair matted, cheeks tearstained, and looked more frightened than Kendra had ever seen anyone. "Where did you come from?" she asked. "What are you doing here, sweetie?"

There were no neighbors, no houses for miles. As she thought about it, an idea grew. Kendra held her stomach as the feeling of nausea rose.

The girl pointed to the barn. "I was trapped in there. I just want to go home."

Poor innocent girl, Kendra thought, trying to keep from crying. She reached out her hand. "Will you show me? I won't let anyone hurt you."

The girl shook her head. "No. I don't want to go back."

"I'd like to see," Kendra said, but the girl wouldn't budge. "Okay. Can you tell me your name?"

"Molly."

"Molly, I'm Kendra. Let's go inside and get you cleaned up, and I'll take you home."

"I don't want to go inside. I want to call the police—my parents. I want to get out of here. Please."

Kendra's heart tore at the broken look in her eyes. "I promise. I'm going to help. Come with me. The phone is inside."

The girl took Kendra's outstretched hand, following her into the house. Kendra got her settled down in one of the upstairs bedrooms.

"You'll be safe in here for now. I'll make some calls."

"He won't find me, will he?"

"No, honey," Kendra choked.

Kendra went back downstairs to figure out what the hell she was going to do. She was done being kept in the dark, done being manipulated. She was going into that barn to see what the hell was going on.

KENDRA SEARCHED, but it didn't take her long to find the small room where the young woman had been kept. There was no sign of physical mistreatment, but from the looks of her, Kendra thought there was also no knowing for sure until she spoke with Molly about it.

She had an idea—a terrible, frightening one. *What am I going to say to Seth?* she wondered. *Is he going to want to kill me for knowing his secret?* Kendra felt like a cornered animal, ready to lash out at Seth the moment he came home. She had to do something with the girl—Molly—but if she took her home, then what?

Seth would go to jail. She might even go to jail. *I have to do it. It's the right thing to do,* she told herself. What other option was there? And yet—she had second thoughts.

Goddamn Seth for putting us in this situation! she thought.

Her mind made up, Kendra resolved to act before Seth could come home. He would stop her—or he would try to, and she couldn't let that happen.

CHAPTER FIFTY-ONE

I look at Christina through the rearview mirror. So blonde her hair almost looks white, so small she almost looks like she'll disappear into the seat. *She should be in a car seat.*

"How far away do you live?" she asks.

"Not far. A few more minutes."

"I should've told my mommy goodbye."

"She was sleeping, remember?"

"Oh." Christina presses her nose to the window, mesmerized by the passing landscape.

I don't scold her for getting greasy fingerprints on the window. I'll just have to remember to wash them off later—if there is a later. "I have a—daughter. She'd love to play with you."

Christina brightens. "Really? What's her name?"

"Her name is Nicole. She's been lonely lately, and I'm sure she would love to have a new friend."

"Me too!" she cries. "I asked Mommy and Daddy to send me to school, but they said I'm too young still. I have to wait until next year even though I just had my birthday."

"That's a shame. How old are you now, Christina?"

"Five!" she cries, holding her hand up to the mirror with fingers spread so I can count them all. She sounds so indignant I could almost laugh. This little miss reminds me so much of Kendra.

"Well, five years old sounds old enough to me. I'm sorry they won't let you go to school. But I'm glad I met you today because now you get to come visit me at my home."

"And meet Nicole."

"That's right."

We make it home without incident. I open the garage to check for Kendra and see her car. She's home alright.

I open the back door on Christina's side. "Hey, do you want to play a game?"

"I thought that's why I'm here?" she asks, looking confused.

I laugh. "Of course it is. Okay, here's the game: I'm going to go get Nicole and you stay here so we can surprise her."

"Like hide-and-seek?"

"Yes, sort of."

"I'm the *best* at hide-and-seek!" She grins at me so I see a gap where she's missing one of her front teeth.

"Great," I say. "I'll be right back. Stay down until I come back."

"Okay!" She climbs down to the floor of the back seat and curls into a little ball.

I gently close the door, lock it from the inside of the front passenger seat, then head toward the house to find Kendra.

IT TAKES me a while to search the house, checking behind every corner, expecting Kendra to pop out and kill me at every turn. The first floor is clear. I move upstairs, avoid tripping over the cat, and find that the second floor is clear too.

There's only one other place she would be. *The barn.*

Before I go down to see Nicole, I know I need to address the problem of no bullets. Yes, I still have the knife. And I could overpower Kendra—*probably*. I'll ignore the number of times that I've failed to do so.

But the point is—I don't want to get trapped down there again. A knife is messy and if there's a struggle—

I stand in the barn, considering my options. I can either stand here all day thinking about it, or I can get my ass down the stairs and do something. *Time to act, Seth.*

With the knife gripped tight, I move to the secret door that's not so secret. I spend a minute moving some of the storage boxes out of the way, pushing the heavier ones farther back in the horse stall. It might only buy me seconds, but I'll take those seconds gladly. When the area is clear, I head downstairs.

KENDRA IS THERE, as expected. She and Nicole look up at me as I come down the final steps.

"Ladies."

"Hi, Seth." Nicole smiles.

Kendra grips her hand. "I'm taking her with me."

"I don't think she wants to go with you, dear."

Kendra turns to Nicole. "It's okay. Tell him how you feel."

Nicole bites her lip, looking between us. "Kendra says—"

"No," Kendra says.

"I mean—I think I should go upstairs with Kendra."

I smile. "Are you sure that's what you want?"

She looks at Kendra again, on the verge of tears.

"I'd hate to have anything happen to you or the baby..." I say.

Her lip trembles.

"Seth, don't—" Kendra protests.

I go on. "I suppose you'd like to live on the streets again. That must've been more comfortable than here."

"Stop!"

Tears are streaming down Nicole's cheeks now.

"It's okay," I tell her. "You don't have to go if you don't want to. I won't let Kendra make you."

"You bastard," Kendra hisses.

"I-I'm afraid," Nicole says, looking at her.

"It's okay to be afraid, honey. I'll protect you. Nothing is going to happen."

Nicole looks back to me for reassurance.

"This is up to you. Not either of us," I say, already knowing what she'll decide. She had a hard life on the streets. Even living down here is better than what she was going through.

"I want to stay," she finally says.

Kendra's jaw clenches, but she doesn't protest. Her eyes find the knife in my hand, the dried blood, then she looks up to see the silent question on my face. It kills me, knowing what she'll do. She objected last time, but last time was different. Last time I didn't know about Christina.

"I met someone new today," I say.

"Who was it?" Nicole asks.

Kendra's face remains neutral.

"A little girl named Christina."

"That's a nice name," Nicole says.

I smile at Kendra. "It's a very nice name. Isn't it?"

Kendra holds her hand out to me.

I raise my eyebrows.

She nods.

I hand her the knife.

And she slits Nicole's throat.

Kendra lets the knife fall to the ground. She stands, sobbing into my shoulder. "What have I done?"

"It's okay," I whisper, holding her, stroking her hair.

"Why did you try to hide her from me? Why didn't you just tell me, Seth?"

"I didn't know what I was thinking at first. Kendra, I was so afraid, so nervous. I knew it was wrong! But she was there on the streets—and so *pregnant*. She needed my help. I didn't know *how* to tell you. I didn't want to lose you."

Kendra dries her eyes, looks at me again. "You were going to keep the baby. For us."

"Yes."

"She wasn't the first."

"No."

"What happened to them?"

I press my lips together, unsure how to tell her. I know she must think the worst of me, but it's not what she thinks. "It didn't work out. They—didn't want to stay. A couple figured out what I had planned... a couple of the babies didn't—" I sigh. "It doesn't matter now. It just didn't work."

After a pause, Kendra says, "You told me you didn't want kids."

"I had to tell you that, don't you see, Kendra? All those miscarriages were killing you! I couldn't let you do that to yourself. Even the doctors warned us that your body couldn't keep going through it. It just—wasn't meant to be."

"Wasn't—"

"And you kept trying to get pregnant, didn't you? Even when I wouldn't do it, you kept at it." I try not to let the anger and hurt cloud my emotions, but it's so hard. Even now, all these years later, with Mark—and probably others—she's still trying to get her precious baby. If she had only known what I was doing for her.

"It wasn't your call to make. It still isn't!"

"I'm your husband!"

Kendra turns from me, crying again. "Our wedding day—"

"That was the first. I really did have a surprise planned for you, but I had to stop her, and then she killed herself. It was a mess—I couldn't tell you, don't you see?"

"All I ever wanted was a child," she chokes.

"I know, wife. I brought you a new one. Finally."

"Christina."

I nod.

She wipes her eyes and face on my shirt. "I thought you would kill me when you found out I knew. And then I thought you'd kill me when you found out about Mark."

"Is that why you tried to kill me first?"

"That—and because you tried to hide them from me. I was afraid. I didn't know what to think—then, well—I figured it out. But, Seth—" She glares at me. "You hid this from me."

"I'm so sorry, Kendra. And I swear I never touched her or anyone else. It was for a baby, that was it."

"I know. And I should've talked to you about it, but I was just so—" She lets out a deep sigh. "Angry. I was hurt and frustrated, and I wanted—"

"A baby."

"Yes. Are you mad? About Nicole?"

I kiss her. "Let's go get our new little girl. The one you picked for us. She's waiting."

CHAPTER FIFTY-TWO

As a master hide-and-seeker, Christina, of course, hasn't moved a muscle. Kendra and I find her in the back seat of the truck, still huddled in a little ball on the floor. When I open the door, she uncurls herself, crying, "Surprise!"

I grin. "Hey, that was great!"

She looks past me and sees Kendra. "Hi, I remember you."

Kendra smiles. "Hi Chris, how are you?"

"Fine. Where's Nicole?"

"She's—feeling tired," I say. "She might play later."

Christina's face falls. "Okay. So what do we do now?"

"Are you hungry?" Kendra asks. "We can make some cookies."

"Yeah!"

The three of us move into the house. Kendra keeps her busy while I sit at the kitchen island and watch them cook, my eyes watering. My wife and child cooking together—something I've wanted to see for I can't remember how long.

Kendra's eyes are watering too. She wipes them discreetly so Christina won't notice. They work together like world-class chefs—mixing and rolling and laughing the entire time. Flour is all over the kitchen but we couldn't care less.

As they work, a thought comes back to me, making nausea rise up my esophagus. *It's not over yet.* I yawn, feeling the exhaustion still pulling at me. *I feel the same.* Nothing has changed—the loop is still here. I can feel it.

It doesn't matter that Kendra no longer wants me dead, that magically we're a happy family again—even better than before. It doesn't matter that I killed four—no, *six* people today. And sacrificed Nicole and her baby... none of it has made any difference.

I watch them with a false smile, the nausea getting worse. I feel like I could puke all over the counter. *Because maybe—even with all those people dead, I didn't kill the right one.*

My breath starts to come in short bursts, almost like I'm having a panic attack. I take a deep, steadying breath to calm down and that's when my chest tightens. I start to massage myself, trying to ease the tension, when it dawns on me what's happening.

I laugh out loud. I can't help it.

Kendra smiles up at me. "What's so funny?"

I'm having another goddamned heart attack! "Nothing. You guys are two peas in a pod, that's all."

She grins.

"What's that mean?" Christina asks.

"It means we make a good team," Kendra says.

Pain radiates through my chest. It's getting harder to breathe, but I try to hide it as best I can. Kendra is too absorbed by Christina's presence anyway, and I'm glad.

I wonder if in another universe—another life—maybe we make it. Maybe we live on together to be a happy family. Or, even better, in another life, we had a child of our own and never had to kidnap someone else's. Maybe I never got that DUI and we were able to be foster parents in yet another life.

Maybe, maybe, maybe.

Maybe I'm not stuck in a loop there either, forced to do something I really don't want to do. Maybe I'm a coward in this life. Because when I fall off the barstool, all I can think is how glad I am that I don't have to do it yet.

"Seth? What's wrong?" Kendra says, rushing to me.

The pain is too much now. I can't speak, even though I want to tell her to keep making those cookies. To ignore me and focus on Christina while she has the chance.

Sweat trickles down my face and runs into my eyes. I hold an arm against my chest, trying to put counterpressure against the tension. *Not much longer now.*

Kendra's eyes are wild. She bends to me and pats the sweat from my face. "Seth, what do I do?"

"Nothing," I rasp.

She glances back toward Christina, still occupied with cutting cookie dough. Before she can speak again, I'm gone.

CHAPTER FIFTY-THREE

I can't believe I actually got her to the point where she didn't want me dead. It's—a miracle. But even with that miracle, I'm back in bed, staring at my bedroom ceiling. All that work—Nicole—Christina—*everything* is gone.

There is one person left, though. The only one who really matters in the end. Kendra.

All those years, all the arguing, the unhappiness, the *trying* —if I kill her now, is that it? No more loop, no more *wife*? No more family. I just have to go on, live the rest of my life without her because I don't deserve to have her?

I hold a hand over my heart, remembering the pain of my second heart attack. Before I give in to my exhaustion and remain lying here until she kills me again, I get up, and I get the knife and the gun. She watches me with those distrusting eyes, but I try to put her at ease as much as I can.

"I have something to tell you," I say. "It's going to sound—a little insane, but I need you to just hear me out."

Kendra only glares at me.

Taking her silence as a go-ahead, I run a hand through my hair, trying to put together the right words. "There's really no way to sugarcoat this. Um—"

"Just spit it out."

"Okay." I pause. "You kill me. You have been killing me over and over and over, and I keep waking up. I'm stuck in this time loop, and everything I've tried to get out of it—has failed."

"A time loop. You can't be serious."

"I know how it sounds, trust me. But think about it. How else would I know where you hid the knife and the gun?"

Her lips tilt like she wants to laugh, but she actually takes the time to consider what I'm saying. "You knew where they were because you knew what I had planned," she says like I'm a child.

"And how did I know the plan?"

"Nick."

I actually laugh out loud at that. "Do you realize it's taken me so, so, *so* long to figure out who the hell Nick is! I had no idea you were talking about Nicole. How am I supposed to know you even knew about her!"

She tilts her head, a smirk still on her lips. Before she can come up with another explanation, another way this couldn't possibly be what I'm saying, I spit out what I know she can't dispute. "I know about Mark and why you're seeing him. I know about Christina."

A look passes over her face—shock and something darker. "I don't know what you're talking about."

"Don't do that, Kendra. Dammit, be real with me for once in our marriage."

"Are you fucking kidding me? You're telling *me* to be real?"

"Look, I don't want to argue. I just want to explain to—I don't know. I want you to understand."

"Understand what, Seth?"

That's the rub of it, isn't it? "I have to kill you now," I say, gripping the gun a little tighter. "I don't want to. Please believe me."

"No one is making you do it. This is your decision, so no, I don't believe you."

"It's the only way to end this loop. If I kill you—sacrifice the most important person in my world, it will finally stop."

"Seth, how the hell do you know that's going to work? You're speculating. You have no way to know, and if you're wrong, if you're having some kind of psychotic episode—"

"I'm not!"

"But what if you are? Seth, you don't have to do this. There's plenty of time to talk this over."

There's something about Kendra that always makes me second-guess myself. She has this authoritative tone, this *I know every goddamn thing and you don't* vibe that is alluring. I do start to second-guess myself. Even after everything, even knowing without a single doubt that this is *real*, I doubt for a split second.

What if she's right? I'm having a breakdown, imagining things, hallucinating? Oh my god, what if I've actually killed everyone— killed Nicole for real? What if Nicole doesn't even exist?

The thoughts run through my mind like a train about to derail. I shake my head to clear the nonsense. *No*, I tell myself. *I'm not having a mental breakdown. The loop is real.*

I'm tired, impressionable, and frankly—heartbroken. There's nothing in the world I want more than to curl up in that bed with Kendra and hold her, comfort her, apologize for being an idiot for all these years. Such an idiot. I can't do those things though because it's time to kill her.

I start to raise the gun when Kendra lunges from the bed. I shoot. The bullet misses Kendra and hits the window instead. Glass and rain spill onto the mattress, but I'm too busy trying to dodge her to care.

She grabs hold of the bedside lamp and throws it at me. She misses, the lamp shatters on the floor. I shoot again. It hits, but only her shoulder. Kendra screams her fury in a high-pitched battle cry.

I realize I still have the knife in my other hand. It's awkward trying to use it left-handed, but when she comes within distance, I swipe at her, and it keeps her at bay for now. "Stop, Kendra," I beg. "I don't want it to be like this."

"I'm not going to die lying down. I'm not going to make this easy for you," she says.

She's going for the door now, but I can't let her. I take aim, step on shards of broken porcelain, and scream. My step falters, but I shoot anyway. Rapid fire, once, twice, three times.

Kendra stops and turns toward me. I can see the holes leaking blood. I rush to her and catch her as she falls. "I'm so sorry," I whisper while rocking her. I wish there was any other way. I don't blame her for fighting.

She fades away in my arms.

CHAPTER FIFTY-FOUR

Nothing happens. Everything is the same. Kendra's blood continues to spill from her open wounds. My heavy eyes threaten to close for good, and all the while, I imagine fate laughing its ass off at my pain.

I look down at her body, drained of all life. *Maybe I still need to die?* The decision is easy. Killing her didn't work—either killing myself in addition will do the trick, or it won't. I take the knife and end it.

CHAPTER
FIFTY-FIVE

Still alive. Back in bed. Next to Kendra.

It might just be me, but the rain sounds louder than ever now. I'm out of ideas. I don't know what to do anymore. I tried killing everyone. I tried killing Nicole—Kendra—*myself*. What more could there possibly be to give?

There's only one explanation that my brain can grasp. There *is* no way out. The loop is infinite, and this is my fate. This really is hell, and I'm never getting out.

I roll onto my side to face Kendra's back. After a moment, I reach a hand out to touch her. "Kendra, are you awake?"

She turns over. "What's wrong?"

"Don't kill me, okay? I just want to tell you something."

"Wha—"

"Just—listen for a minute."

She seals her lips closed, waiting for me to continue.

"I want you to know that I love you. I'm sorry for everything we've been through, every shitty moment, every cruel thing I've said or done. You are the light of my world, and I still love you through it all."

Her bottom lip trembles. "Why are you saying this to me?"

"Because I don't know if I'll get the chance to say it again, and I want you to know."

"You already know what I have planned." It's not a question.

I give a silent nod in the dark.

"Did you call the police?"

I pause. *The police*—Megan and Nick asked me about calling the police too... I never did because of Nicole. Well—and because I didn't want Kendra to get taken away. I knew—at least I *thought* I knew, I would find a way to stop her.

The police are the one thing I haven't tried yet. What if that's the answer I've been looking for?

"No," I finally say. "I didn't call them."

"Good," she says. And with a move so fast it barely registers, she gets the knife and slices me wide open.

CHAPTER
FIFTY-SIX

Once again, I don't give myself time to think. There is no thinking here—only acting. I open my eyes, reach beneath Kendra's pillow, grab the knife and the phone. Then I move to my nightstand to get the gun.

I leave the room, dialing 911 on my way out. I turn it on speakerphone so I can still use the flashlight to see my way down the stairs. I'm on my way down the stairs when the automated system places me on hold.

The next minute, Kendra is running after me. "Seth! Hang up!"

I cross the house, ignoring her. If I have to put up a fight, I will, and it might even be better if I do.

"Seth! Don't call—"

"9-1-1, what is your emergency?"

"My wife is trying to kill me! Please send the police."

"What is your location? Do you need an ambulance?"

Kendra steps into the kitchen. She stares at me, unmoving, unblinking, waiting for me to answer.

I open my mouth to answer.

Kendra shakes her head.

"Sir?" the operator says.

"I'm here. I'm not hurt, but I don't know if that's going to change before anyone gets here."

"Police are on their way. Can you get to a safe place?"

Kendra turns from me, bolting back upstairs. I don't know what she has planned now, but it doesn't really matter anymore. They're coming now. She'll be in jail—taken from me, but not dead. *And she should be in jail*, I remind myself. After all—she was willing to kill Nicole so easily. She was willing to kill *me* so easily—so many times. Yes. This is the answer.

"I'm safe now," I tell the operator. "I have to go now, or she'll hear me." I end the call to wait by the front door.

With nothing but the sound of the rain and lightning, I almost fall asleep on the couch while waiting for the police to show up. The house is eerie downstairs. Dark and silent— shadows looming from every corner, staring at me, waiting for my next move.

A sound comes from the stairs. "Kendra?"

She doesn't answer. Instead, I hear a faint scratching noise. Then—a low, slow *growling*.

"What the—Kendra!" I stand from the couch, staring wide eyed in the direction of the sound. I'm waiting for her to step out toward me with a foaming mouth full of rabies, but she doesn't.

Sirens are in the distance now.

The stairs creak. Either Kendra is going back up or finally coming all the way down—whichever it is, the growling stops.

I open the front door, step outside, and raise my hands. "She's inside!" I cry as officers come forward.

"Gun!"

"Drop the gun!"

I look up at my hands. I was too distracted on my way out to realize I still have the gun and the knife. I let them fall to the ground, and an officer comes to handcuff me. "I'm just detaining you until we can figure out the situation," he says.

I go with him willingly and watch as the others enter my home. I keep a close eye on the barn—none have gone that way yet, but I'm sure it's just a matter of time. They'll find Nicole, and I'll have to give Kendra the credit for her too.

Time passes. Finally, they bring out Kendra kicking and screaming. My heart tightens at the sight of her being dragged out of our home, and for a moment, I'm afraid I'm having another heart attack. I force myself to take deep breaths. In... one, two, three... out... one, two, three... repeat. Just a little anxiety, no heart attack.

"Check the barn!" Kendra screams.

The officers shine a light toward the barn doors. "What's in the barn?" one asks.

"My husband has a girl locked up in there. Go see for yourself."

"My god, Kendra! You have a girl in there! Please, someone, you have to save her!" I yell, trying my best to look disgusted.

There are enough officers here to separate Kendra and me, each in our own separate squad cars, and still have more to check the barn. They search and search, they bring in more lights and search some more. An officer comes back to speak with Kendra when they can't find anyone. She forgot to mention they'd have to look for a door in the floor.

An officer stands alone next to her open door. He leans

over to speak with her—I can't tell what. Whatever she says to him, he decides to get her out from the back seat of the squad car and lead her to the barn. *I don't like this. Not at all.*

The two of them walk closely as they cross the driveway. I can see her train of thought before *she* does. Within five seconds, she begins to struggle with the officer. He calls out for backup, but before anyone can react, she gets hold of his gun.

She doesn't shoot him like I thought she would. Instead, she points it at him and makes him let her go. And he does, looking confused because—it's not like she's going very far.

Everyone waits on pins and needles to see what she'll do. With her gun toward the cop, no one wants to risk losing an officer's life. Kendra backs away—back toward me—keeping her gun aimed at the officer.

When she finally reaches my door, she opens it.

"Kendra, don't do this."

She turns toward me and blows my head off my shoulders.

*L**et's try that again.*

I wake up, get the knife, the phone, the gun. I leave the room, using the phone as the flashlight—waiting to dial 911 until I get downstairs. Only when I'm by the front window, with the light of the storm behind me, do I finally call. Again, the automated system places me on hold.

Kendra doesn't hear because they're not on speaker. She doesn't cry out for me to hang up or chase me downstairs. It begins to dawn on me exactly how silent the house is—

"9-1-1, what is your emergency?"

I clear my throat, but I don't have to try to sound worried—it comes naturally. "My wife has a knife. She's trying to stab me."

"What is your location? Do you need an ambulance?"

I try to listen for her footsteps, but there's nothing but the sound of the storm outside. "Yes, send an ambulance and tell them to be careful. She's dangerous!"

"Police are on their way. Can you get to a safe place?"

"I'll try. I have to go now, or she'll hear me." I end the call, but instead of waiting near the front door again, I walk halfway up the staircase. I strain my ears, trying to listen for the scratching noise that came before, the *growling*. But there's nothing. *Maybe it was just the cat.*

"Kendra?" I call up toward our bedroom.

She doesn't answer.

I wait, debating whether or not to try calling to her again. I know she's still in the bedroom, but why is she being so damned quiet? Why hasn't she come after me?

I hear the sirens. The police are approaching the driveway now. I come back down the stairs—remember to drop the knife and the gun—then step through the door with my hands up.

As they shine their lights on me and come forward, I run through a list in my mind. *Did I remember everything?* I remembered to drop the weapons; I warned them that she was dangerous—even though they should've known that! I think that's it...

"Are you hurt? Who attacked you?" an officer asks.

"My wife—she's inside. Be careful!"

"Does she have a gun?"

"Yes! A knife too."

A few officers file into the house while I'm led away to the police cars and ambulance. The paramedics look me over while I keep a close eye on the house—and the barn. Kendra isn't going to go down without a fight. She hasn't yet, and she's not going to now.

After some time, an officer comes back through the front door. "She's not here," he tells me.

"She has to be. It's dark—she's probably in a closet or something. Did you check everywhere?"

"There are still officers inside. You didn't see her leave the house?" He nods to the barn. "Maybe she went in there?"

"I don't know. No. I didn't see... but you know, she does like to go out there a lot. She could be there."

He gets on his radio to communicate and call for more backup. Some of the officers have baton lights, but they may need night-vision goggles to find her. The search in the house continues until eventually a K-9 unit arrives, and they enter the barn.

A HIGH-PITCHED SCREAM echoes through the night, followed by screams of the officers. Goose bumps run up my arms at the sounds. The dog barks. Shots are fired. There's an invisible scuffle inside the barn. It all happens in a heartbeat, with almost no time to react.

The officers with me put me in the back of a squad car and close the door *for my safety.* They make some calls on the radio, then they head toward the chaos, leaving me alone. The paramedics remain but they're tucked away too, waiting to see what will happen.

The same thought flashes in my mind. *I don't like this. Not at all.* The only thing I can do is wait.

AFTER WHAT FEELS LIKE AN ETERNITY, officers bring Kendra from the barn. She's being carried—bleeding, screaming—a wild beast that I don't recognize. She struggles in their grip but there are too many of them this time and she doesn't stand a chance.

No one follows with Nicole, and I know that she's dead. The scream was hers. They found her—just, too late.

"You're not pinning this on me!" Kendra rages. "You hid this from me! You're not living happily ever after while I'm locked away, Seth. I won't let it happen!" She actually growls at me through the window as they pass to another squad car.

I do feel guilty because, yes, I am going to pin everything on her. And I'm going to lose her. But I don't feel guilty about the part where she tried to kill me. *That* part was real, and she deserves to be punished for it. But only if it ends the loop.

As I sit, watching the activity outside, waiting for someone to remember that I'm still trapped back here, a strange feeling overcomes me. *Is this really happening?* I have a moment's doubt, thinking this entire thing might be a hallucination—a product of my lack of sleep.

The loop is real—there's no question. But what if I'm not really sitting in the back of a cop car with my wife being arrested and taken away? What if I'm still up in that bedroom, too tired to open my eyes, and I've passed into some kind of alternate reality?

My mind reels with the possibilities. I could be in a loop within a loop—within another loop even. I shake my head, not wanting to think of it anymore. *You're going to give yourself an aneurysm, Seth, and reset everything before it's finished.*

Finally, I see Kendra through the back of another car, being driven away. Another officer comes to let me out and take my statement. I give an abridged version that they'll be able to believe, then he says, "You're free to go. We need to do some forensics in the house and barn. Can you get a hotel?"

I get the keys to my truck and head to the hotel in town.

CHAPTER FIFTY-EIGHT

I feel almost—naked. I have no wife, no Nicole, can't go home—I'm alone. Everything I love has been taken from me, and now I'm supposed to... what? Move on? Live my life?

I'm not sure how much forensics they have to do out there in the barn, or what exactly they saw or didn't see, but I have a feeling even with Kendra behind bars, I'm not going to get off scot-free. I kept things tidy out there but not tidy enough to withstand a microscope. Maybe they won't look that close—or maybe they will.

It dawns on me that this might not be the answer either. All this tonight—for what? To pin my mistakes on my wife? Nicole is dead along with the child. Our family is more broken now than ever. This can't be the answer... can it?

I pace my hotel room, waiting to feel some kind of sign that this loop is over and done for good—that this *was* the right choice, the key to ending it. I still feel dead tired, like I could sleep for a year and still not have enough. It's not a good sign. Shouldn't I feel some sort of magic? Or just—I don't know, a shift?

None of those things have happened. I'm not sure if they

will or not. There's only one way to know for sure because this time, I'm not going to kill myself.

The bed stares at me from across the room and I stare lovingly back. "You're waiting for me, aren't you?" I say with a faint smile. I plop down on the bed, fully dressed—not even bothering to take my shoes off. I close my eyes, and within a few heartbeats, I drift off to sleep.

Well, bad news. It didn't work. I'm back in bed—at home, next to Kendra. The storm is still raging on and on like it hasn't stopped even for a second.

Part of me is actually relieved. I have everything and *everyone* that I care about back. Kendra is alive and here, Nicole and her baby too—a twisted little family *whole and alive.* Sadly, it won't be like this for long. Because now I know what I have to do.

It took me so long to see it, but I guess that's the point of a journey, isn't it? I suppose that was the purpose of the loop. To teach me to see what was right in front of me. To teach me that instead of trying to convince myself that I'm doing the right thing, to own up—to admit when I've done something wrong. To take credit for it instead of trying to pin it on someone else.

I sit up in bed, get the knife, the phone, the gun. I only get them because I need my wife to not murder me before I can get out of the house. I'm not going to kill anyone this time, either. I almost wish that was the answer—*I would kill them all*—but by now, I know that it's not. Been there, done that. Didn't work.

I don't want to keep waking up only to be murdered by my own wife. I don't want to keep feeling this sinking, endless exhaustion that never goes away, unable to sleep for eternity. I don't want to see that look in Kendra's eyes anymore, or all the other horrible things. And Nicole's voice when I come down those steps to see her—

This is it. The only solution.

So, one last time, I make my way downstairs, grab the truck keys, and head into town.

THE POLICE DEPARTMENT only has a couple of cars in the parking lot at this hour of night. I've never been here before, don't know what I'm doing, but figure it can't be that hard to turn myself in. *Are you sure about this, Seth? You could hire an attorney first—*

No. No attorney, no skimping on this or trying to make it easier on myself. I did the crime, and now I'm going to do the time. Besides, even if I did want one, how the hell would I really get one? I can't go to sleep, or I reset. If I wait—I'll never be able to make it that long.

I cross the parking lot to the door. It's locked. I pull again —harder. Still locked. I lean forward to read the sign that says, *Open to Public 8am-5pm. Please call 911 for an emergency or 555-0150 for the nonemergency hotline.*

Well, shit. Still standing there, I pull out Kendra's phone— luckily, I don't have to unlock it to call 911.

"9-1-1, what is your emergency?"

"Yeah, I need to report a crime."

"What is the nature of the crime?" Her tone is impatient, almost pushy, and gives me a moment's pause.

"I need to confess. To kidnapping—and murder."

"What is your location?"

"I'm at the police station. I didn't know where else to go, but the doors are locked—"

"Is anyone with you now? Anyone injured?"

"No. It's just me. I'm fine."

"What's the location of the person who is injured?"

"No one is injured. They're dead. And they're buried in the forest. Look—"

"An officer has been dispatched to your location. ETA five minutes."

Two officers show up. They're actually pleasant considering the call that they just received. They take my statement, advise me about getting an attorney, and place me in handcuffs. They're almost shocked at the situation—one even says he's never seen someone call 911 to confess like this and at this time of night.

"I couldn't sleep," I say. "It was eating away at me."

"I hear that," he says, leading me back to the police cruiser.

"Isn't this the jail? Where are we going?"

"Sorry, buddy," the other officer says. "Our holding cells are full tonight. You picked a bad night, my friend. All the town drunks are out and about. We're going to head over to the county jail to get you situated."

They help me into the back seat of the car, and then we head toward the county jail. When we get there, we pass through a guard station and a secure gate before we get to the back of the building. As the officers escort me out of the car and inside to booking, one says, "It's going to be a long weekend, Seth. But come Monday, a detective will probably want to have a good long chat with you."

I only hope that I'm still here by Monday. I almost laugh out loud at the thought—wondering what he would say if I told him how I felt. He probably wouldn't do anything other than look at me like I was crazy, but that's okay. Maybe I am a little crazy by now. And I know one thing—if I wake up in bed next to Kendra again, I'm not sure how long it will be before I really am batshit.

CHAPTER SIXTY

It's an odd feeling. Not really being in prison, behind bars—that, yes, of course, but that's not really what I'm talking about. I'm talking about confessing. Telling the truth—the whole, absolute truth about something I did.

It's—liberating. And I know how that sounds, trust me. But it's the truth. *The truth will set you free*, isn't that what they say? Whoever *did* say that sure knew what the hell he was talking about.

I feel like twin boulders have fallen from my shoulders. I feel like an invisible foot has been pressing gradually harder and harder on my lungs, trying to stop me from taking in more air. Now—I can breathe. I'm free, even with the bars in front of me. The feeling that *this is right* fills my being.

"Hey guy, what the hell are you grinning about over there?" someone calls to me.

I straighten my face. "Nothing, just thinking about my daughter."

"No fucking funny business, right?"

I don't know what funny business he's thinking of, but I definitely don't have any in mind. I'm going to be here for a long, long time, *with any luck*, and I'm not starting off by making enemies.

I yawn so hard I feel like my jaw could dislocate. My eyes water. "Hey—do you know where I can—"

He points to an area with bunk beds. There are no private cells here—at least, all the private ones are taken. I know what they say happens in prison. I know what happens to the first guy who falls asleep. I'm new—fresh meat—but I'm about to fall asleep standing up.

If someone attacks me while I'm asleep—I guess that's fate's last laugh. If I get out of this loop, I'm not sure how much I'll mind. I'll have to let you know in the morning—if I'm still here.

I feel their eyes on me as I move to an empty space. I sit, only hoping that it's no one's spot. The other beds have personal belongings nearby but not this one, and I'm too tired to give it a closer look. If someone tries to wake me up, I might kill them with my bare hands.

I lie down. My head touches the flat pillow. And I pass into oblivion.

CHAPTER SIXTY-ONE

Back from her morning walk, Kendra checks her mailbox on the way up the driveway. Inside, a letter from the penitentiary sits along with a few pieces of junk mail. *Another letter from Seth*, she thinks, grabbing the stack.

She had to spend a year of her life away from him once when he got the DUI. Now Kendra is going to be parted from Seth forever. A confession without recanting—no trial, no defense, only life in prison, and she can't forgive him for it.

She wanted the satisfaction of having his blood on her hands, feeling his pain, seeing his surprise, but now she would never have that opportunity. *At least he's where he belongs*, she thinks, wishing she knew what made him confess. Confessing isn't in Seth's nature. He was always one to blame other things or other people, never own up to what he'd done. This was the rest of his life, and he just—gave it away.

She tosses the stack of mail in one of the outside garbage bins before going inside. Upstairs, she showers and redresses. She goes back downstairs to fix a meal when the phone rings.

Kendra checks the caller ID—then answers, "Hey, Nick. How are you?"

"I'm in hell," he says with a shaky voice. "Have you been able to get anything out of him?"

"Not yet. I'm so sorry, Nick. I wish there was more I could do to help."

"Have you looked everywhere? I mean—I know the police did, but—"

"Trust me. They tore this place from top to bottom. *I* tore this place from top to bottom too. There's no sign of her here. And if there was, don't you think I'd be the first to tell you? She is my best friend."

"I'm sorry. I know." He starts to cry. It makes Kendra uncomfortable, but she lets him go on. "God, I miss her so much!"

"I do too," Kendra says.

"The baby was due last week, you know."

"I know."

"We were going to name her—"

"Don't do this to yourself, Nick. We're going to find them. They're not gone forever."

Nick chokes back a sob. "I hope you're right."

"I am. I feel it in my bones. We're going to find them both. *Alive.*"

"I'm sorry to keep bugging you. I just thought, maybe—"

"You're not bugging me, and I'm glad you called. You're my friend too, not just Megan."

"You were—*are* a good friend to her, Kendra."

They say their goodbyes. Kendra goes back to making her morning meal. She's still getting used to the feel of the empty house, and she's glad it won't be empty for much longer.

When her meal is finished, she heads out to the barn.

THE DOORS CREAK open as she enters and flicks on the lights. Seth's workstation is lit, along with the horse stalls full of storage containers. The police made a mess of things when they pulled Nick out.

She went home, telling everyone how Kendra tried to help her. The police did their search for evidence, making even more of a mess of the place, but since then, Kendra has been able to put things to rights. It looks almost like nothing had happened at all now.

Kendra crosses to the back of the barn where the not-so-secret latch is. She moves the boxes stacked on top, lifts the door, and climbs down. In the small room below ground is her friend Megan on the bed, writhing in labor pain.

"How are you feeling?" Kendra asks.

Megan shakes her head. "Please, Kendra, let me go. I need a hospital."

"I'm sorry, Megan. I can't do that."

Another contraction racks through Megan. She screams with the pain, gripping the sheet so tight it tears beneath her fists.

Kendra moves to check her progress. "You're nearly there," she says.

"I can't do this. I can't do this here!"

"You don't have a choice."

Megan bears down with each new contraction until it's time to push. She pushes and screams and pushes some more, sweating and crying, and cursing Kendra.

Kendra takes one of Megan's hands and pulls it down

between her legs so she can feel the top of the baby's head. "She's right here, Megan. You can do this."

With another scream, Megan pushes again with all her might until she finally feels a great gush leave her body. She falls back onto the mattress, wholly drained, as the sound of the baby's cry fills the small room. Barely able to stay conscious, she watches Kendra hold and clean her baby.

Tears welling in her eyes, Kendra coos to the little bundle so small and tiny. "Hello, little one. You are so beautiful." The memory of the girl—Molly—surfaces.

Things didn't work out with her. She kept trying to escape, fought tooth and nail, then she lost the baby—Kendra felt for her, maybe more than most. She tried to connect with the girl, make her understand she wanted no harm to come to her, but she just wouldn't understand. Kendra wasn't sure what Seth thought happened—maybe that she went back to the streets, maybe that she got out and just died. The girl did die eventually—in the upstairs bedroom that Kendra kept locked. The one Seth never bothered trying to enter.

Megan attempts to lift her arms. "Give her to me," she croaks.

Kendra ignores her. Her job here is done; it's time to leave. She turns toward the stairs, the baby still in her arms. "I'm sorry, Megan. Nick is gone. I didn't want this, but Seth left me no choice."

"Nick? Who—don't say that to me. Don't do this, Kendra! We're friends! I would do anything for you!"

Kendra continues up the narrow steps back into the barn. "And now you're giving me a child of my own."

Megan keeps screaming behind her, a guttural, feral cry, until the door to the room is closed once again.

Kendra looks down at the child in her arms—her child. Her heart swells with happiness and love. This is everything she's always wanted, and now it's finally hers. *If only Seth would've been smarter. If he wouldn't have lied to me, tried hiding*—she cuts the thought short. There's no more room for regret and anger in her life. What's done is done.

She brings her new baby daughter into the house to show her her new nursery upstairs. Megan is left in the barn—forgotten. Kendra will worry about moving her body another time. For now, she only wants to welcome her child into the world.

THANK YOU

THANK YOU FOR READING!

For a behind-the-scenes look at a deleted chapter, sign up for the K. Lucas newsletter at:

https://BookHip.com/WFXNZZF

Enjoyed You Kill Me?

Please consider leaving a review.

Reviews help authors more than you might think. Even just a few words make a difference and are greatly appreciated. The best place to review is whichever retailer you purchased from, but you can also consider Goodreads or BookBub.

Shadow, the cat—furious at being yelled at, trampled over, and otherwise disrupted from his comfortable position on the top step of the stairs, slinks through the dark corners upstairs, thinking about revenge. His hackles are still puffed, tail still stiff and painful from the mistreatment, and he releases a low growl, full of irritation at the human who can't figure out how to leave the house. The woman has gone after him now, and Shadow hopes she catches him—he hopes she is able to complete what she's set out to do.

At the end of the upstairs hallway, he sulks to the corner of an open doorframe, where he kneads his claws against the wood. He relishes the feel beneath his paws, digging deeper and faster to release his anger. Shadow whips his tail back and forth, emitting a slight purr, and slowly, his irritation passes. His dark-gray fur smooths out once again, and he blends into the shadows for which he was named.

Something catches his eye. He stops. His body is frozen in time except for his wide yellow eyes that follow the movement so minuscule a human would've missed it. His left ear twitches, his whiskers tingle.

At the top of the doorframe, a spider, smaller than the tip of a kitten's dewclaw, stands in the darkness, stretching its legs. It skitters forward, then stops. It waits, sensing that it's being watched.

Shadow stares, unblinking at the arachnid that would be invisible if not for his superior vision. Even for a cat, he can see, hear, and sense more than others. His perked ears pick up the sound of the spider scratching itself, rubbing two hairy legs together. Shadow waits patiently, claws now retracted but still resting against the wood.

The spider, no longer sensing danger, continues hurriedly across the top of the doorframe and down its length. It pauses again, nearly to Shadow's paw, that's lifted a fraction of an inch from the wood. It waits, tucked in close to the doorjamb to stay unseen. All clear, the spider continues the rest of the way to its impending doom.

A split second before Shadow snatches the arachnid up and crunches its exoskeleton between his jaws, licking the remaining guts from the tips of his talons, the spider releases a signal to its comrades. The remaining cluster of spiders, believing the area to be safe, comes forth from the depths of the house, and Shadow, satisfied he's caught his prey, decides he's too tired to deal with this new problem—he'll leave it for someone else to take care of.

Hundreds upon hundreds of tiny spiders crawl across the house, branching out across the roof, walls, and floor, in search of food of their own—and for *Mama*.

ACKNOWLEDGMENTS

As always, I'd like to thank my husband and son for being my biggest fans and supporters, always offering me encouragement when I need it the most, and being so understanding about my deadlines. I love you both to infinity and beyond.

Thank you to my editing team, at My Brother's Editor, for being so amazing and for everything you do. I can't tell you how lucky I am to have found you!

Thank you to Angie, for helping me create the perfect blurb.

To my cover designer Dez, at Pretty in Ink Creations, thank you for making me the perfect cover to represent this story.

To my readers, you and your continued support mean the world to me! Thank you for sticking with me, for encouraging me, fanning the flames, and for picking up each new book that releases.

Thank you dear reader, for showing me your support by reading this book. Whether you are new to my work or are one who keeps coming back for more, I truly hope you enjoyed the read.

ABOUT
K. LUCAS

K. Lucas is a bestselling author who lives for the unexpected twist. Originally from California, she now lives in the Pacific Northwest with her husband, son, dogs, cats, and chickens. After earning a bachelor's degree in information technology, she became a homeschool mom and then a full-time author. She loves all things thrilling & chilling, and her favorite pastimes include reading, watching scary movies, and exploring nature.

www.klucasauthor.com

CONNECT WITH
K. LUCAS

See K. Lucas's website for more info, signed copies, and to sign up for newsletter updates!

www.klucasauthor.com

To support future projects, get EXCLUSIVE behind the scenes content, sneak peeks, and more, find K. Lucas on Patreon.

patreon.com/klucas

amazon.com/author/klucas

goodreads.com/klucas

bookbub.com/authors/k-lucas

instagram.com/author_klucas

facebook.com/author.klucas

tiktok.com/@klucasauthor

pinterest.com/klucasauthor

twitter.com/AuthorKLucas

www.ingramcontent.com/pod-product-compliance
Lightning Source LLC
Chambersburg PA
CBHW030401200726
48286CB00015B/2248